Fourteen Jewish Flavored 10-Minute Plays

David K. Farkas

V. 12-30-24

ISBN
Paperback: 978-1-7367012-3-2
Ebook-Kindle: 978-1-7367012-5-6

Dedication

I dedicate this book to my very good teachers during the time of my life, 1st through 12th grades, when good teachers were few and very important to me. To

- Miss Moses (with love and deep gratitude), 4th grade.
- Miss Stefanacci, Math, 5th grade.
- Mrs. Jagel, Science, 7th grade.
- Miss Katz, who became Mrs. Tiedrich. History, 10th grade.
- That crazy biology teacher whose name I've forgotten, 10th grade.
- Mr. Zuluski, Debate Club, 11th and 12th grade.
- The remarkable Miss Ritchie and Mr. Grosse, English, 11th grade. Miss Ritchie was dismissed after fall term; Mr. Grosse was dismissed after spring term.

Acknowledgments

I gratefully acknowledge the very astute and creative individuals who carefully read and critiqued the manuscript that became this book: Charles Blank, Susan Blank, Jean B. Farkas, Lenny Hort, Joan Stern Kato, Marty Levine, Rabbi Nina H. Mandel, Josh Mendel, and Roy E. Schreiber. I also wish to acknowledge the very helpful reviews my scripts have received by those who participate with me in Donna Hoke's Trade a Play Tuesday (TAPT).

Credits

The book's cover graphic derives from "Clockmaker" (1914) by Yehuda Pen. The ice cream cone photograph is by Donald Erickson, licensed from iStock. Ziaul Haque contributed his expertise in graphic design, book design, and digital publishing.

Table of Contents

Al Farkas is a sales rep for a furniture manufacturer during the Great Depression. Al wonders how long his friend Abe Goldberg will be able to keep his run-down little furniture store afloat. Then the opportunity of a lifetime walks through Abe's door—but Abe is reluctant.

Al Farkas is a sales rep for a furniture manufacturer during the Great Depression. Al wonders how long his friend Abe Goldberg will be able to keep his run-down little furniture store afloat. Then the opportunity of a lifetime walks through Abe's door—but Abe is reluctant.

It is 1965. Seth tells his parents that he is going to drop pre-med and become an environmentalist—a field almost no one has heard of. Seth's friends are baffled. Far worse is the reaction of Seth's deeply disappointed parents and Seth's uncles and aunts. Still more trouble awaits on campus. But Seth finds an unexpected ally who strengthens his resolve.

It is 1963. David is a bored, restless senior at a high school where the spirit of conformity rules. David and some classmates are driven to hysteria and rebellion in the school's language lab. Retaliation is swift and violent. The play is a prequel to "She's a Runner."

David is finishing a pleasant visit with Betty, his beloved great aunt. As he is leaving her senior residence, Betty takes him aside. She has a special request. All her life, Betty has sought, but only sometimes found, her freedom. Today may be her last chance. She doesn't mind breaking the rules.

What We Preserve

Years ago, Sam and Gabe were partners—big-time real estate developers in Florida. Now they're both retired. Sam enlists Gabe for one more deal—bigger than anything they'd ever done. This time it's not for the money, but for their children—one living, one dead. Gabe is ready to take on the corrupt state legislature. But he doesn't foresee all that lies ahead.

Proof of God

It is 1976. David has just moved to Lubbock, Texas. He learns immediately that life is going to be very different—especially because he's a Jew living amid people who have never met a Jew and think of Jews as figures from the Old Testament. Things start a bit rough. Will life in West Texas work out?

Sally from the Bronx

It is 2009, and Sally Silberman Farkas, my mother, is being buried today. Family members, friends, and a rabbi are gathered at the gravesite for some remembrances and the funeral service. But being dead is not going to stop Sally from commenting on everything that's going on around her.

Sunday Walk in North Creek Park

Dan is a social disaster, a schlemiel who gets nothing right. He is well meaning, but lacks judgment and social restraint. He will always speak when he should be quiet and then say the wrong thing. What should have been a pleasant walk with his wife goes very wrong.

Perspective

watercolorist who is painting a seascape at a beachfront park. Along comes Morris Rifkin, a working-class Jew with a grievance about his station in life— plus the age-old Jewish instinct for arguing. Walter's painting did not come out quite as he wished, and he's about to tear it up. Says Morris, "What right have you to destroy a painting that others would enjoy?"

Butterflies

Dr. Alan Aronowitz, a Freudian psychiatrist, cannot figure out how to treat his patient, Mr. Farrell, who is convinced he's surrounded day and night by fluttering butterflies. In desperation, Alan and a colleague devise a bogus psychiatric treatment supposedly based on the Kabbalah.

Afterword

I relate how my relationship to Judaism changed as I put together this collection of plays and wrote the postscripts

Reference List

Bibliographic references for works cited, plus some helpful annotations.

Introduction

To provide context for the plays in this collection, I will tell you a little about me and my family background. Then I explain how this book is organized. Finally, I suggest that folks get together to perform these and other 10-minute plays as a recreational activity—as I do with my family and friends. Part of this discussion is a look at copyright law.

Welcome to my life

I am an American Jew, more cultural than observant. I was born in 1947 in New York City. My brother, Mitchell, is two years younger. In our early years we lived in the middle-class Stuyvesant Town housing project in Lower Manhattan. In 1956, the family made the big move to the New Jersey suburbs. We lived in a handsome split-level in the brand new Rolling Hills subdivision in the city of Clifton. We were just a 40-minute drive from midtown Manhattan, and we often attended Broadway musicals and plays.

My grandparents were Eastern European immigrants who saw no future for Jews in their countries. My father's family is Hungarian. (My middle name is "Kalman.") My mother's family is Russian. They lived in the Bronx and Washington Heights. Both families achieved the bottom rung of the middle class. The children did better still.

Al Farkas, my father, became a successful furniture salesman—a manufacturer's rep who sold inexpensive bedroom sets to furniture stores in Brooklyn and northern New Jersey. Most of the stores were small. Many were owned by Jews.

Sally Silberman Farkas finished secretarial school and went to work for a small Jewish-owned fabric business. She became a homemaker when she married Al, just back from the South Pacific, in 1945.

We all attended services on the High Holy Days and fasted on Yom Kippur. Even so, we were essentially a secular family. My Jewish upbringing, like that of many largely assimilated Jews, was full of contradictions—which I fully recognized. Mitchell and I got small Hanukkah presents each night after we lit the Menorah and sang the blessing. But our Christmas presents were the big ones. Christmas stockings were OK, but there was no Christmas tree. Santa Claus was prohibited because he was a saint. But not wanting her children to be deprived because they were Jews, Sally bought every Frosty the Snowman decoration she could find in the stores.

The only two aspects of Judaism that aroused passion in my father were support for Israel and not marrying outside the religion. He was a shrewd stock market investor, but bought lots of Israeli bonds, despite the low return and high risk of default. Al refused to attend the wedding of a favorite niece because the groom was not Jewish. But this was a man who didn't attend services except on the High Holy Days and never referred to God, the Ten Commandments, or heaven in a conversation. You could look everywhere in our home and not find one artifact that indicated a religious affiliation.

I did a good job (as everyone told me) at my bar mitzvah. In 1964 I was sent off to the University of Rochester with the plan that I would become a doctor. Very quickly, my parents were deeply disappointed when I switched my major from pre-med biology to English. Ultimately I became a university professor. In 1968 I married Jean Blank Farkas. Jean was raised in a kosher household. Her father had been president of their synagogue. Because I'd married "a nice Jewish girl," my parents were batting one for one. But Mitchell kept them waiting a long time. Sally and even my father accepted Gail, an Episcopalian, as Mitchell's fiancé, but only because Gail was undeniably a great woman and because Mitchell had waited long enough that they desperately wanted to see him married.

Over the years I have belonged to various synagogues, but I've also gone long stretches without membership in a synagogue. Even so, I am deeply Jewish and most pleased to be a Jew. Why? Because Jews have always respected education and learning; because Jews love to talk and argue; because modern Jewish ethics are predominantly pragmatic and socially focused; and because American Jews have been strongly Liberal/Progressive and Leftist. There is one further and very important reason: It is extraordinary to be part of a group of people who have maintained their identity and traditions—under some of the worst possible circumstances—for so very long.

Our daughter, Eva, married Adam, a non-religious Protestant. Our grandkids, Jonah and Hazel, consider themselves both Jewish (Passover and Hanukkah Jewish) and Christian (Christmas and Easter-egg Christian). This modest degree of Jewish identity would not fully satisfy my father, but both kids do consider themselves Jews. So, that's my personal and family story.

About this collection

The title of this collection reads "Jewish Flavored" so as not to overstate the Jewishness of these plays. I am not remotely as Jewish (or remotely as talented) as Sholem Aleichem, Isaac Bashevis Singer, or Bernard Malamud. If my plays connect directly with any readers, they will be cultural Jews. But beyond this direct connection, I hope these plays, along with the postscripts that follow each play, will interest and entertain readers regardless of their religion or lack of religion.

The time period in which the plays are set extends from pre-history (a retelling of the story of Adam and Eve) to the Middle Ages. Then, Eastern Europe in the 19th century. The rest take place in the United States in the 20th and early 21st centuries. I've sequenced the plays roughly by the chronology of the setting. There are actually fifteen plays in this collection. I've included "La Paloma"—a play without a Jewish connection—because it is a prequel to "She's a Runner."

Each play is followed by a page or two of commentary. These are the postscripts. The postscripts make clear the meaning of each play, and in many instances relate the circumstances in my life or family history on which the play is based. The postscripts are interwoven—meaning that ideas introduced in one postscript may be picked up in a later one.

As I wrote the postscripts, some of my ideas were uncooperative and wanted to go off in their own direction. I gave them permission to do so. Therefore you will find embedded within the postscripts these nine mini-essays:

- Jewish Ethical Traditions
- Anti-Semitism
- Jews and Italians
- Jews and "Walters"
- Jewish Florida
- The Stay-at-Home Wife
- Jews and Medicine
- Arguing Jews

The collection, much to my surprise, sprouted a brief afterward section. As I was wrapping up the project, I realized that my relationship to Judaism had changed, and so the book seemed incomplete without a few pages explaining this change.

Taken altogether, the scripts, the postscripts with their mini-essays, this introduction, and the afterward can be read from beginning to end as a single literary work, often highly personal, in which Jewish beliefs and culture (and my own life) are examined in many ways.

Stage directions

It is said that when theater directors study a script they are planning to stage, they often ignore all but the most basic stage directions. Directors are creative artists, and they want to think through for themselves what the script means and how they will interpret it. However, at the risk of annoying any directors who may look at these scripts, I've provided detailed stage directions. This is because I prioritize the casual reader who is reading the script just one time. I want that reader to fully envision the play as it might be staged.

Recreational theater

Perhaps some casual readers of this collection would like to become amateur actors, directors, or playwrights. You will find that performing 10-minute plays with a group of friends is a great social activity. Jean Farkas and I have led an informal little theater group since June 2019. We are a group of friends, most of us seniors, centered in the small Seattle suburb of Lake Forest Park. We call ourselves the Goat Hill Theater Company. We rehearse lightly and perform four 10-minute plays, script-in-hand, for friends and family in such venues as the community room of a local library and a church basement. During the worst of Covid-19, we performed outdoors in the warm months.

My Kindle-published book *Performing 10-Minute Plays with Friends* fully explains how to organize your own recreational theater group. My other Kindle books (besides this one) are *Writing the 10-Minute Play* and *Academic Life in Sixteen 10-Minute Plays*. My special hope is that *Performing 10-Minute Plays with Friends* will encourage folks to form their own recreational theater group and that *Writing the 10-Minute Play* will encourage some folks to write plays for their theater group.

YouTube videos

During the early years of the Goat Hill Theater no one thought to make videos of our performance. In fact, there are just a handful of photographs. Later we began making very basic smart-phone videos. Here are links to the videos of the plays included in this book:

"Butterflies": https://youtu.be/tVeJ0rCe9jg

"She's a Runner": https://youtu.be/4dAuOHUIf4w

"Proof of God": https://youtu.be/GAyL1IO9_wk

"Perspective": https://www.youtube.com/watch?v=2z_JTmR9hMQ

"The Rabbi and the Banker" (two performances):

https://youtu.be/--rWZGjIIKA
https://youtu.be/tZVn2aW0qIA (play starts at minute 8)

Copyright considerations

To help people launch their own recreational theater group without having to think about permissions and royalties, I put the scripts of nine of my 10-minute plays into the public domain. Few playwrights do this. Those nine scripts, titled the Jumpstart Collection, are included in *Performing 10-Minute Plays with Friends*. The Jumpstart Collection can be freely downloaded from the internet as a DOCX file at www.pwcenter.org and as a PDF file at www.newplayexchange.org. Search for "Farkas" or "David K. Farkas." Copying a Jumpstart script from the Amazon Kindle digital edition of *Performing 10-Minute Plays with Friends* is possible but very awkward. Because the nine scripts in the Jumpstart Collection are in the public domain, anyone can copy them, modify them, and perform them (even if you sell tickets) without paying royalties.

The scripts in *Fourteen Jewish Flavored 10-Minute Plays* are (except for "The Expulsion from Eden") fully copyrighted. Therefore, the purchase of the book does not include performance rights. However, copyright law in the United States exempts strictly private performances. You and a group of friends can perform any of my plays or anyone else's plays as a private social activity without paying a royalty. In much the same way, you can legally pick up a guitar and sing a hit song to friends gathered in your living room. This exemption, however, is lost for any kind of public performance—for example if you advertise in any way or if you charge for the performance. I explain copyright issues in greater detail in *Performing 10-Minute Plays with Friends*.

If you are interested in obtaining performance rights for any of the plays in *Fourteen Jewish Flavored 10-Minute Plays*, except for "The Expulsion from Eden," contact FarkasWords-LLC. (farkaswords@gmail.com). The response will be quick, friendly, and helpful. The licensing will be inexpensive. I will also send you the script you've chosen as a file in DOCX format. "The

Expulsion from Eden," is in the public domain because I included it as a Jumpstart play in *Performing 10-minute Plays with Friends.*

The Expulsion from Eden

A 10-minute play by

David K. Farkas

I place this play in the public domain. Anyone is welcome to distribute, perform, modify, or expand upon the script of this play. – David K. Farkas, 2020.

Dedicated to Professor Katherine Koller Diez.

Characters:

Adam
Eve
The Angel Raphael
Cain
Meraltic: Cain's trusted messenger
Enoch: Cain's son
Narrator

Suggested minimum casting:

Adam
Eve
The Angel Raphael/Narrator/Meraltic/Enoch
Cain

Setting:

Eden. The harsh world beyond Eden. Nod, the nation ruled by Cain. No sets necessary.

[Scene 1]

ADAM and EVE enter from opposite sides of the stage and confront each other. They each wear a loose, hastily constructed garment, something like a toga or perhaps just a light blanket. RAPHAEL, resplendent in appearance, watches from upstage, but gradually steps forward and into their view.

ADAM: Why are you covered?

EVE: I did not want you to see me naked. And you?

ADAM: The same.

EVE: Everything is changing.

They approach RAPHAEL with shame and trepidation, their heads bowed. Then EVA tries to resume her former relationship with RAPHAEL.

EVA: Oh, Raphael. Tell us about these things that are happening . . .

RAPHAEL: Stop! We no longer speak familiarly.

Startled and appalled, ADAM and EVA step backward.

RAPHAEL: If you have a question, you may ask it.

ADAM hesitates.

RAPHAEL: I said, if you have a question, you may ask it.

ADAM: Raphael, what do we call these coverings we now wear?

RAPHAEL: You will call them "garments." Adam, Eve, you will no longer need to ask me such questions. Your minds are now filling with new thoughts and words.

EVE: Like death?

RAPHAEL: Like death. You now know sin and shame, suspicion, discord, and more. You will soon see death in many forms—including murder. You will know toil, pain, and illness. And you will need to find your own answers, for when you leave Eden, you will see me no more.

ADAM: This will happen soon?

RAPHAEL: Yes, very soon. You have just minutes to absorb the meaning of what has happened and to ready your minds for a world that is complex and threatening—nothing like what you've known. Adam, the beasts are no longer your friends, especially at night. You must cut a stout branch and sharpen one end so that you can ward off predators.

ADAM: Woman, you have caused all this woe!

EVE: I did nothing.

ADAM: You ate of the apple. Is that nothing?

EVE: The serpent was subtle. He lied.

ADAM: Why did that matter? There was one commandment, just one. Do not eat from the Tree of the Knowledge of Good and Evil. That's all you needed to know.

EVE: The serpent tempted me. He spoke of knowledge like it was something I should want. The apple had a bright glow like no other fruit I'd ever seen. That glow made me hunger for its taste. Then, after I ate, I was afraid, and I could not stand to be alone in my fear and dread. So, I offered the apple to you in order to join our fates.

ADAM: Stop! . . . We needed only to obey that one law and Paradise was ours forever. Now we must suffer and die, and our children must suffer and die. They will curse us—especially they will curse you.

EVE: *(After a long pause.)* Yes, they will curse me. I have caused great harm, never to be equaled. Adam, do you still love me? Am I not still lovely to look upon?

ADAM: You are less so. You are now mortal, and this can be seen. But that is not the point. Oh, Eve! Mother of sin and sorrow. I hate and despise you for what you have done.

EVE: Adam, I would gladly take the full weight of God's punishment upon myself alone. Then you might remain in Paradise.

RAPHAEL: This is not possible. Adam ate. He could have refused, but he did not.

EVE: *(To RAPHAEL.)* But I brought the temptation to him. I told him how the taste opened my mind, expanded my vision.

RAPHAEL: If Adam had refused, there would have been no Fall, no punishment—just a warning and further instruction. To fall, you needed to fall together, and you did.

EVE: Adam, you did eat, but I tempted you. And not just with my words. My breasts, lustrous hair, waving softly in the breeze, have often led you to comply with my desires. No different this time. Adam, if only I could, I would die so that you could remain in Paradise.

ADAM: *(Softening.)* You would. I know that.

EVE: Perhaps God would give you another woman, someone better than me. You would tell her, "Once I had a woman named Eve, but she was evil."

ADAM: These thoughts are too terrible to speak of.

RAPHAEL: *(To ADAM.)* Is Eve entirely to blame? Think, Adam.

ADAM pauses and is stricken.

ADAM: Eve, I was commanded to watch over you. For our mutual safety, we were not to be long apart. But I let you stray far enough from me that I could not hear the serpent speak to you. I am also at fault for what has happened.

RAPHAEL: Yes, Adam. Yes. Think *further,* Adam.

ADAM: *(Looking closely at EVE.)* I am sorry for blaming you as I did. You are Eve still, and I love you. Whatever may befall us, I will cherish you.

RAPHAEL: Yes, Adam. *(To both ADAM and EVE.)* Time is very short, and I must help you prepare for life outside Eden. Adam, you have learned the most important lesson: Forgiveness. Eve has learned it too. In Eden, before you fell, love was easy. You loved each other, you loved the animals who greeted you each morning. They loved you. But forgiveness is much harder than love. Forgiveness comes after you've been hurt, and you *will* hurt each other in words and in deeds. So will the future generations. Therefore, you must practice forgiveness and teach forgiveness to your children.

ADAM: I understand: Forgiveness quells anger. And I understand more. If I see a young deer sinking in soft mud, and I pull it out, that is kindness. If an animal tries to steal our food, and I set down my spear, that is mercy. But forgiveness is hardest, for it comes when I have been injured.

RAPHAEL: Forgiveness comes hardest. But it heals.

EVE: Adam, I know some things you do not. I tell you that forgiveness comes more easily to women than to men. Someday I will joyfully forgive my new babes for the pain of childbirth. And my daughters will forgive their babes, even as they lie bleeding to death in childbirth. The woman, in her last moments, will ask to hold her babe. In her last moments she will ask her husband to forgive the child for the loss of his wife. In their last moments together, the woman will instruct her husband to love the babe and teach it well. And men shall heed.

ADAM: Raphael, what more can you tell us in the short time we have left?

RAPHAEL: Evil has been set loose upon the world. There is evil within you, and evil is now part of Nature. Your descendants will know pestilence, wildfire, and floods. They will know envy and cruelty, crime and plunder. The future generations will be born into a battle they can never win—but which they can easily lose—if they succumb to cruelty or despair. But you can push evil backwards and enlarge the precious space in which good flourishes. Adam, Eve, history now begins. The world lies all before you.

ADAM and EVE turn toward RAPHAEL, then toward each other.

RAPHAEL: *(Gesturing.)* You must go now. This way.

ADAM and EVE take each other's hands. They exit.

[Scene 2]

ADAM, as a middle-aged man, holds a farming implement. EVE, as a middle-aged woman, carries a basket. They are dressed simply, as farmers, perhaps in clothing that was hidden under the flowing garment each wore in Scene 1. CAIN holds a weapon.

ADAM: Cain! To kill your brother, our son. The Angel Raphael warned your mother and I that terrible things awaited us outside of Eden. But this is beyond what we could imagine. I don't know how we will keep on living, but I know we must.

CAIN: Father, why was Abel's sacrifice preferred before mine? Why?

ADAM: I do not know.

EVE: But was this cause for murder? The murder of your brother.

CAIN: Oh, I am the most wretched among men. I despise myself. The first murderer—and such a murder it was! My own brother, who loved me.

EVE: Cain. Understand this: We forgive you this deed. We must if we are to go on with our lives.

CAIN: I deserve no forgiveness. I deserve curses. I deserve your curses each day of my life.

EVE: We forgive you, son. You are our son. Despite all, you have our love.

ADAM: It is not enough that we forgive you. You must learn to forgive yourself. You can earn this forgiveness through kindness and generosity and working to heal the world. And by teaching others what you have learned. Teaching, teaching our children, this is our greatest hope. It's our best way to grow the army that fights evil on the battleground of daily living. Do you understand me, Cain?

CAIN: Understanding does me no good, Father. Even now I have a strong impulse to slay and replace you. In my wicked thoughts I am the husband of your widow, who is my mother. I am deeply evil, so deeply evil! To keep my desires in check, I must run off to the wilderness and live alone.

ADAM: Then do so. Subduing the evil within you is virtue. But it is not enough. It is only the first step toward building a virtuous life.

CAIN: How can such a thing be possible for me?

EVE: It is possible. Some day you will return from the wilderness.

CAIN: I am too sinful. Too weak.

ADAM: You must try. How else can you live?

EVE: Yes. You must try. Remember, you have our forgiveness and our love. Let this be the foundation for a better life.

[Scene 3]

The NARRATOR, reading from a Bible, enters upstage.

NARRATOR: And Cain spoke: "I shall be a fugitive and a vagabond on the earth. And anyone who findeth me shall slay me." But the Lord answered, "No" and set a mark upon Cain as a warning to all not to kill him. And Cain went out into the wilderness, and he settled east of Eden. And Cain knew his wife, and she conceived and bore Enoch. And Cain built a city in the desert.

The NARRATOR exits. EVE, now much older, enters. MERALTIC enters.

MERALTIC: I bear a message from Cain, your son.

EVE: *(Astonished and joyful.)* Adam! Oh, Adam! Come here. Something wondrous. A messenger from Cain. *(To MERALTIC.)* Is he well? Where is he living? It has been many years.

ADAM, walking with a cane, joins EVE.

MERALTIC: Yes, Lady. Your son is well. He lives in Nod, a city that he founded and governs. He is married to Trafelsa. His son is Enoch. I am Meraltic, Cain's trusted advisor and friend. He would have no ordinary messenger speak to you.

ADAM: Founded a city? How could this be?

MERALTIC: After many years of wandering, both through the desert and in his mind, he made peace with himself. Soon after, he found his goodness and his strength. He then gathered many followers. Nod is a populous city that has established many trade routes. It is guarded by walls, high and strong. Cain is much honored. But he has heavy responsibilities, so he could not take time for the long journey from Nod to where you dwell.

EVE: He waited all these years to send us news?

MERALTIC: He waited until he could show you the life he lives now, his family, and everything he's achieved.

EVE: He was foolish. We would have rejoiced to receive any news—any news other than his death.

MERALTIC: I understand. He told our people about his terrible sin. But it is very hard to face the parents of the son you murdered. He thanks you deeply for your forgiveness and unshakeable love. He has taught forgiveness to Enoch, and to many others. He governs with wisdom and always with mercy. Can you visit him in Nod?

ADAM: Alas, we are too old to travel.

MERALTIC: Perhaps a day will come when he can be absent long enough to visit you.

EVE: If we never see him, this is still a joyful day for us.

MERALTIC: I am very weary. Let me and my attendants withdraw to our tents. We will return in the morning. I will tell you much, and you will tell me much that I can relate to Cain.

ADAM: Yes. Please. Of course. Until tomorrow.

MERALTIC exits.

[Scene 4]

EVE: Adam, what will be our last thoughts as we die? What *should* they be?

ADAM: That we have lived well . . . and would have been happy except for the memory of our original sin and of Abel's death. What the world will say of us, we cannot know.

EVE: We will be blamed. I especially.

ADAM: Sometimes I have strange thoughts. Sometimes I think, dare to think, that it was good we left Eden and struck out on our own. A baby sucking at his mother's breast is in Paradise. But is that living? Were we truly living? Perhaps our sin was a kind of birth, a birth into the adventure of life. Perhaps God was in league with the serpent. Perhaps God and the serpent are one and the same. Raphael was our teacher while we lived in Paradise, but the serpent truly opened our eyes. Perhaps this is how life should be lived.

EVE: These are indeed strange thoughts.

[Scene 5]

CAIN is seated on a chair that suggests authority and respect. ENOCH is standing.

ENOCH: Father, there is unrest. Some say that your mercy toward the Cimmerians is weakness, the softness of a woman, not acceptable in one who governs a city and leads an army.

CAIN: They must learn otherwise, Enoch. We must show mercy. We must forgive the Cimmerians their foolish attempt to conquer Nod. We must teach them to live in peace with us, to join our trading caravans.

ENOCH: Of those who govern cities and nations, few think as you do. Is this because of Abel? Is this your atonement?

CAIN: The Angel Raphael taught forgiveness to my parents, and that was their gift to me. Abel also. As he died from the blow I struck, he said, "Brother, for this evil deed you will know terrible guilt. But, when the time comes, you will be able to rebuild your life. In doing so, you have my blessing." In the depths of my sin, his words meant nothing to me, but as I began to recover myself, they gave me strength. So, having been sustained by such forgiveness, how can I not extend mercy and forgiveness to others? How can I not teach these things?

ENOCH: I understand, Father.

The End

Postscript to "The Expulsion from Eden"

The story of Adam and Eve from the Hebrew Book of Genesis has been hugely influential in Western culture. However, like many of our myths and legends, it is a bare-bones narrative. For example, little is said about the emotional lives of Adam and Eve, either before or after they eat the apple. Scholars can add explanatory footnotes and detailed commentary, but to work as fiction, the mere 1200 words that Genesis devotes to Adam and Eve must be elaborated upon. The greatest retelling of the story, John Milton's *Paradise Lost,* is a poem of about 11,000 lines.

For a play that runs just 10-minutes, "The Expulsion from Eden" tells a big story. I follow Adam and Eve out of Eden, through their mature years, and into old age. Genesis says almost nothing about Cain's later life other than that he had a son and built a city. In Jewish interpretive tradition neither Cain nor his city do well (Ginzberg, 2003). But I depict Cain as a man who redeems himself from his sin and lives a successful life.

Borrowing from *Paradise Lost,* I show how the loving relationship between our First Parents collapses into anger and recrimination after they partake of the apple, but survives, largely through Eve's generosity of spirit and love for Adam. But this deeply troubled couple gets help. The Raphael of the play, like Milton's Raphael, is the world's first marriage counselor and a very good one.

The Romantic poet and visionary William Blake, commenting on *Paradise Lost,* famously said that "Milton was of the Devil's party without knowing it." Blake's insight explains how Milton was able to endow Satan with such fierce energy. But it also points to the idea that the human adventure could not have taken place within the protected confines of Paradise. Human history and human greatness required the fall and expulsion from Eden. This idea finds its way into my play:

> **ADAM:** Sometimes I have strange thoughts. Sometimes I think, dare to think, that it was good we left Eden and struck out on our own. A baby sucking at his mother's breast is in Paradise. But is this living? Were we truly living? Perhaps our sin was a kind of birth, a birth into the adventure of life.

I have also infused the play with what I regard as one of the best parts of modern Judaism. When Cain confesses his terrible impulse to slay Adam and possess Eve by force, Adam tells Cain that he is evil only if he carries out his evil desires. Subduing the evil within him is virtue. This idea is further discussed directly below in the mini-essay "Jewish Ethical Traditions."

Finally, I deeply believe that forgiveness, not love, is the pre-eminent virtue. It's easy to love when someone or something is lovable. As the Jewish mother says in praise of her lovely daughter, "What's not to love?" Forgiveness is much harder. It comes (or doesn't) after we've been injured, and it asks us to look beyond that injury.

In the play, the lesson in forgiveness that Raphael teaches Adam and Eve leads to their forgiveness of Cain. This and the forgiveness offered to Cain by Abel in his dying moments become Cain's lesson for Enoch and perhaps for us as well. Christians learn forgiveness from the words of Christ as he died on the cross.

Jewish ethical traditions

Philosophers who specialize in ethics speak of three predominant ethical frameworks: deontic ethics, consequentialist ethics, and virtue ethics. Jewish ethical traditions are complex and partake of all three of these frameworks. All three are present in this play.

Deontic ethics are based on rules and obligations. Traditional Judaism is heavily deontic (Dorff & Crane, 2013). We are required to follow God's commandments and Jewish law. The prohibition not to eat of the apple is deontic, and deontic ethics carry weight in the play. Doesn't God have the right to make a rule, to establish some limit to Adam and Eve's freedom of action? More broadly, God is giving Adam and Eve the opportunity to exercise their virtue through choice. From a contemporary perspective, following God's commandments, for example, by observing ritual, creates a holy space in our lives.

Consequentialist ethics are social. They look at how actions impact people. Contemporary Jewish ethics (along with much secular ethical thinking) is consequentialist. But there is also a strong consequentialist element in traditional Jewish ethics. For example, during Yom Kippur, the most holy of the High Holidays, it is necessary to resolve your conflicts with other people before you can reach to God to atone for your sins. ("Jewish views on sin," Wikipedia, 2021).

In the play, it is from a consequentialist perspective that Adam speaks to Cain about the need to heal the world (Tikkun olam). Then, when Cain confesses his evil impulse to kill Adam and take Eve by force, it is again from a consequentialist perspective that Adam tells Can there is virtue in controlling this evil impulse. Through an act of will, Cain has avoided doing great harm. But Adam makes clear that more is required of Cain than simply suppressing his evil desires—which leads us to virtue ethics.

Virtue ethics are holistic. They ask us to become a moral person. Traditional and modern Judaism follow virtue ethics because we are called upon to imitate the goodness of God (Blau, 2000). Virtue ethics tends to challenge and broaden deontic and consequentialist ethics. If, following deontic ethics, you adhere mechanically to the precepts of your religion, virtue ethics asks for something beyond simple obedience. Similarly, in the play, it is from the perspective of virtue ethics that Adam tells Cain that resisting his impulse to do harm, while virtuous, is still not sufficient. It is only *the first step* toward building a fully virtuous life—which Cain does.

The play, then, accords with both traditional and modern Jewish ethics in drawing upon all three of the primary ethical perspectives.

Malachi in the Time of Plague

A 10-minute play by

David K. Farkas

Written in April 2020, in response to the coronavirus pandemic.

Setting:
The great hall of the castle of Count Leonid, ruler of the principality of Jurn, in the region of Rozgony (now part of Romania), during the Middle Ages.

Characters:
Malachi: An aged Jew, a physician.
Count Leonid: Ruler of Jurn.
Archdeacon Dorin: A church official in Jurn.
Father Grigori: A prominent priest in Jurn.

Suggested minimum casting:
Count Leonid
Malachi
Archdeacon Dorin/Father Grigori

[Scene 1]
COUNT LEONID is seated. MALACHI BEN AVRAM stands before him.

COUNT: Rabbi Malachi. Are you and your daughter well settled in your quarters? Have you eaten?

MALACHI: Yes, My Lord. Thank you.

COUNT: Your daughter, what is her name?

MALACHI: Rebecca.

COUNT: It must have been most difficult for you and your daughter to cross the mountains this time of year. You are not . . . a young man.

MALACHI: Yes, it was difficult. But Rebecca was a great help, and the snow was not as deep as we expected.

COUNT: *(Smiling.)* Perhaps your God was watching over you as you crossed the mountains.

MALACHI: *(Smiling back.)* Perhaps so. But perhaps He was watching over everyone who was on the trail with us. Perhaps it was a peasant's donkey He had chosen to protect.

The COUNT chuckles in appreciation, then turns serious.

COUNT: You left the service of Baron Mihal of Oridea. Tell me why.

MALACHI: There were difficulties. I do not wish to say more.

COUNT: I require an explanation. You are in Jurn now, and I rule Jurn. And, as you are a rabbi, I expect a truthful answer.

MALACHI: I will explain, Count Leonid. But, by your leave, I am not a rabbi. I am an educated man, but I am not a rabbi.

COUNT: Of course. Your training is in medicine. Then we will call you "Doctor Malachi." What is your full name?

MALACHI: I am Malachi ben Avram. Yes, I am trained in medicine. I was not trained in one of your universities, but I will answer to "doctor."

COUNT: I know the plague is coming to Jurn and to all of Rozgony. It is not here yet, but there are reports, and I study maps. It will come. It came to Oridea. But tell me: Why did you leave Mihal of Oridea, and in the midst of the plague? Were you afraid of contagion? Were you seeking greater rewards? Surely Baron Mihal was paying you well. Jews are known to have the best treatment for the plague. I need your answer.

MALACHI: I ministered mainly to those in Oridea who were still healthy but lived on streets where others had been infected. For some, my treatment provided protection. Not to all.

COUNT: How have the Jews come to understand the plague?

MALACHI: I think we understand very little, but my brethren have learned to prepare a potion from the dark yellow scabs of those who were infected but survived. Then we give the potion to people not yet infected. Sometimes it protects them. Sometimes it does nothing. Alas, sometimes they come down with the plague in just a few days. But almost all of them would have become ill before long.

COUNT: So, what happened in Oridea?

MALACHI: Baron Mihal's son, Andrei, became very ill, and Baron Mihal was in terrible fear. He told me. "There will never be a patient for whom you will try harder. If Andrei survives, I will give you much gold—500 pyra. If Andrei dies, you can expect to die as well." I answered, "Your threat is pointless. I exercise the same care with every patient—prince or stable boy." Andrei recovered. But I cannot live with such threats, so I made plans for Rebecca and I to slip out of Oridea—not an easy thing to do.

COUNT: What about the gold?

MALACHI: I would have liked the gold, but somehow it was not forthcoming. I do not say that Mihal would not have paid me, but it wasn't coming quickly, and so I took my opportunity to escape from Oridea.

COUNT: Well, I am very glad you came here. Problems will arise. You know that. But I promise you will be safe under my protection.

MALACHI: Thank you.

COUNT: We have our own physicians in Jurn. You will not be welcomed.

MALACHI: I understand. I have dealt with this before. When a patient recovers and I am thanked, I explain that it was the patient's Gentile physician and I—our treatments working together—that effected the cure. If a Gentile physician wishes to learn what I know, I will share.

COUNT: A more serious problem is the Church. When the plague comes and if the people of Jurn are spared from the worst and, especially, if those you have treated are spared, certain priests will proclaim loudly that you brought the Devil to our aid. People listen to the priests, and this will be a problem.

MALACHI: This is a problem that *you* will need to deal with.

COUNT: *(With hardness in his voice.)* Yes, and I will . . . It has gotten late and you are surely tired. You should retire. Good night, Doctor Malachi.

[Scene 2]

COUNT LEONID is seated. FATHER DORIN stands before him.

COUNT: Father Dorin, you know the plague is coming. It will come over the mountains. It will wreak havoc here. I have secured the aid of a very learned physician. He is a Jew. Malachi ben Avram.

DORIN: The people of Jurn have grown up with stories of evil Jews.

COUNT: Father Dorin. You are Archdeacon here. You will make sure that Doctor Malachi is not hindered in Jurn.

DORIN: I have no objection to a Jewish physician practicing in Jurn. Indeed, perhaps on some occasion, perhaps here in the seclusion of the castle, I will be able to meet Doctor Malachi, converse with him.

COUNT: Your personal openness toward Malachi is welcome, but it is not enough. You will make sure that Doctor Malachi is not endangered by the rantings of our clergy. The clergy must *calm* the people.

DORIN: I can make your wishes known. But Father Grigori is a special case. Back when there were Jews in Jurn, Grigori's grandfather had trouble with them, and the family lost its land. He has long spoken out against Jews. His hatred cannot be blunted, and I have no authority over him.

COUNT: *(Standing.)* I need your help, Archdeacon Dorin.

DORIN: I can tell the people of Jurn that I had a vision from God. In this vision, Gold told me that Doctor Malachi has been sent to help us in the time of our travail. I do this with great trepidation. Such an act of false prophecy, whatever the motive, puts my soul in peril.

COUNT: You are a good shepherd, not a false prophet. But will your vision suffice? Will it calm the people?

DORIN: It will do something, but it will not suffice. Father Grigori is a powerful man in the pulpit. I cannot match him. Once Grigori has spoken, your doctor will likely face angry mobs if he ventures out of the castle.

COUNT: Then I will need to do more. We need this Jew, and I promised to keep him safe. I will speak with Father Grigori.

[Scene 3]

> COUNT LEONID and FATHER GRIGORI are standing in a confrontational manner.

COUNT: Father Grigori, it is unfortunate that we cannot come to an understanding. You know that Archdeacon Dorin is willing to have a Jew treat the people of Jurn. We think that the physicians of Jurn will come to accept him. I have offered to address your family's long-standing grievances.

GRIGORI: I don't know how you persuaded Dorin, but you will not persuade me. And you cannot stop me. You may govern Jurn, but you don't have jurisdiction over Church affairs. If Malachi is successful in working his cures, I will attribute his success to Satan. I will say, "Is it not better to die of plague and rise to Heaven than turn to Satan to keep one's life?"

COUNT: Strong words, Father. And I doubt not your power over the people. But I can play a strong game myself. Tell me, is Marius still serving as Head Usher in your church? How strange, after all these years! First he sang in the boys' choir. Then, when he grew older, you found him another role. And now, he is Head Usher. In every other church, this honor rotates among deserving parishioners, but in your church, it is always Marius. Somehow Marius always seems to be by your side.

GRIGORI: I know what you are saying. This means nothing. No one has seen inappropriate behavior in my church. Your accusations will only bring you shame.

COUNT: Father, you are correct. I know better than to accuse a man as holy as you are—as careful as you are. But I must do everything I can for the people of Jurn. Malachi knows a great deal about the plague, and for a sum of 50 pyra he has agreed to prepare a powder so strong that just a few sprinkles on a man's garments will bring on the plague in its deadliest form. If you cause trouble with Doctor Malachi, I promise you that when the plague reaches Jurn, some peasant, some shopkeeper, someone you will not suspect will sprinkle that powder on Marius as he carries out his duties as Head Usher. Marius will not be the first in Jurn to die of the plague, but he will be *one* of the first. And only God knows who might follow, it might even be you, Grigori.

GRIGORI: This is an outrage! You threaten the life of an innocent young man? You are always careful to stay on the good side of the people, but there are those who know how ruthless you are. And Malachi. He will use his skills to concoct a deadly poison? A Jew he may be, but doesn't he fear punishment from his God for such a thing?

COUNT: Father Grigori. Don't express such surprise. Your teachings are familiar in Jurn. *(Speaking now in mocking irony.)* Don't we all know that Jews will do anything for money?

GRIGORI: You are worse than the Jew.

Count LEONID glances offstage as if giving some kind of signal.
MALACHI enters to face FATHER GRIGORI.

COUNT: I hope you do not object if Doctor Malachi joins our conversation. There are no plans to harm Marius, just a desperate need to prepare for the plague.

MALACHI: Father Grigori. Can we not take a step backward from where we are? I do not seek to undermine the Church or your authority in any way. Jews and Christians have lived peaceably together in many places and times. Can we not live together in Jurn? You read our bible as well as your own. Through medicine and faith, the plague can be endured.

FATHER GRIGORI is partially placated.

GRIGORI: The Jews who loaned money to my grandfather were dishonest schemers. Evil men.

MALACHI: This may be. I will not defend people I do not know.

FATHER GRIGORI appears more fully placated.

COUNT: I told you, Father Grigori, that your grievance can be addressed. The money your family lost can be restored . . . It is time for you to make your choice. I do not think you want to face my wrath. Instead, we can work together for the good of the people of Jurn, both body and soul.

MALACHI: We all acknowledge that when people are preserved from the plague, it is because they have prayed in church.

GRIGORI: Count Leonid. The people of Jurn know my feelings about Jews. I will not have them think I've been threatened or bribed. Will you accept silence, stony silence, regarding Malachi ben Avram?

COUNT: That will be enough.

Makes a gesture that encompasses FATHER GRIGORI and DOCTOR MALACHI.

COUNT: We have made progress. We will prepare for the plague.

The End

Postscript to "Malachi in the Time of Plague"

During the height of the Covid-19 pandemic, I had an impulse to write a Covid-themed play. I wanted to depict a leader who acts wisely and decisively to fight the plague, a stark contrast to what we all saw unfold in the United States. I didn't initially intend a Jewish play, but my Jewish heritage often finds its way into my creative imagination. As the outlines of the story took shape, my physician became a Jew. I then knew that anti-Semitism and suspicion of Jewish doctors would necessarily enter the story. As I wrote, anti-Semitism became a larger and larger part of the play.

As a Jewish playwright, I admit to discomfort endowing Malachi with so much virtue. Therefore, I was pleased to moderate Malachi's thoroughgoing altruism by showing that he was interested in the reward

Baron Mihal had promised if Malachi was able to save the life of Mihal's son.

Anti-Semitism

All Jews, I think, are deeply aware of the anti-Semitic attitudes and evil acts that extend far back into the history of Europe and other regions as well. So the fierce anti-Semitism of Father Grigori and the general suspicion and latent hostility toward Jews on the part of the citizens of Jurn struck a chord with me as I wrote the play. But, personally, I have not been deeply impacted by anti-Semitism.

Many—probably most—of my Eastern European relatives were lost in the Holocaust. However, my parents and my extended family in the United States had not maintained close ties with those in Europe, so I did not grow up with an active sense of loss. I feel some shame admitting to this. I've sat with Jewish friends as they sorrowfully displayed photograph after photograph of relatives—people who they'd never met—who died in one or another of the death camps. But my parents talked about World War II, Hitler, and the Holocaust much as American Christians would have. It did not appear to be personal to them—with just one exception: When my parents were wealthy enough to vacation in Europe, they avoided Germany.

My father experienced some ugly anti-Semitism working as a traveling salesman in the South and as an infantryman during World War II (which I tell of later). Also, just after World War II, my father interviewed for and was offered a good job at the Metropolitan Life Insurance Company in New York. However, when he mentioned taking off work for the High Holy Days, everything fell apart. "What? You're a Jew? We don't hire Jews here." He was shown the door.

Al's many dinner table stories included his encounters with anti-Semitism. After a store owned by one of Al's Jewish customers burned to the ground, an acquaintance of my father in the furniture business, not knowing Al was a Jew, suggested that the fire had been caused by "Jewish lightning." This phrase insinuates that Jews set fire to their businesses when they want to collect the insurance. Al did not relate such stories in anger. Rather, he told his stories to help my brother and I better understand the world we were living in. I believe that my parents' overall attitude regarding anti-Semitism was, first, that Jews were doing very well in the United States and, second, there would always be some anti-Semitism anywhere you went.

The Montclair Beach Club is located just three blocks from the house at 200 Chittenden Road (Clifton, NJ), where we lived. The Montclair Beach Club most definitely excluded Jews from membership. I had no strong desire to be a member, but their bigotry did come to mind often during the summer months when I could hear the cheers from their swim meets through my bedroom window. Once when I was at the beach club, as the guest of my friend Rob, Rob pointed to old Mr. Cole, the owner, playing shuffleboard. Rob took me aside and commented, "If he knew you were a Jew, he'd kick you out right this minute."

Many years later, Jean Farkas and I were cordially completing the process of renting an apartment in Minneapolis when, through a chance occurrence, the owner of the building became aware that we were Jews. Immediately, he told us that the apartment was not available. There are other incidents I could cite, but not so many, and none of great importance in my life. Jean and I have friends whose bitterness regarding anti-Semitism is a continuing presence in their lives. If I had more direct and intense experience with anti-Semitism, I would be a different kind of Jewish playwright.

The Rabbi and the Banker

A 10-minute play by

Reuben Asher Braudes (1851–1902) and David K. Farkas

Developed from Reuben Asher Braudes' "The Misfortune: Or, How the Rav of Pumpian Tried to Solve a Social Problem," translated by Helena Frank in the 1912 volume *Yiddish Tales.* (See reference list.)

Setting:

Scene 1 takes place in the shtetl (Jewish village) of Pumpian during the mid-19th century. Pumpian is located in the Lithuanian region of Imperial Russia. Scenes 2 and 3 take place in the sumptuous home of the rich Jewish banker Yaakov Kovner, in Vilna, Lithuania's largest city.

Characters:

Rebbe (Rabbi) Itzhak Nachman.
Devoreh Nachman: His wife.
Yaakov Kovner: A rich Jewish banker in Vilna.
Moshe Kovner: Yaakov's son, in his 20's.
Narrator: Can be played by "Moshe."
Rebecca: Devoreh and the Rabbi's daughter. This is a brief walk-on part that concludes the play

✳✳✳

[Scene 1]

The NARRATOR stands, facing the audience. While he speaks,
DEVOREH enters and sets down two simple meals on a crude table.

NARRATOR: Pumpian is a village in Lithuania. The inhabitants are poor
Jews. There is no railway, no telegraph, and only occasionally does a
newspaper appear to tell the people what's going on in the world.
Pumpian is a very quiet place.

DEVOREH: *(Calling offstage.)* My Dear. Come to lunch.

During the NARRATOR'S next speech, the REBBE enters slowly, hugs
his wife lightly, and sits down to his meal. DEVOREH joins him.

NARRATOR: Rebbe Nachman is the son of the previous rabbi. He is a
good rabbi, who lives a quiet life. He spends much of his time studying
and contemplating the Torah, the Talmud, and other sacred texts. He has
never yet found a reason to travel more than a half hour beyond
Pumpian.

The NARRATOR exits.

DEVOREH: I have potato soup. And some pumpernickel bread.

REBBE: Do you want to know what I have been thinking about?

DEVOREH: Of course, Itzhak.

REBBE: I read from holy books that to be rich is a great misfortune.
Rebbe Osher has written, "Riches are stored to the hurt of their owner." In
the holy Gemara, there is a passage which says, "Poverty becomes a Jew
as scarlet reins become a white horse." There are passages in the
commentaries that say the poor see the world truly, but the rich are
deceived by their wealth. All of us in Pumpian are very fortunate to be
poor.

DEVOREH: Oh, Itzhak, my dear and learned husband. This is excellent
wisdom for a rabbi. But perhaps it does not fit so well with everyday life.
Surely being poor is not such a blessing.

REBBE: Why do you say that?

DEVOREH: It is not good when children do not have enough to eat. Or, a man's horse dies, and he has no money to replace the horse and continue to earn a living. Being poor, we ourselves have our own misfortune. There is no money for Rebecca's dowry.

REBBE: We will find a way.

DEVOREH: But it's two years now. Rebecca wants to be married. She is 19 already. She is a good girl, a rabbi's daughter, a pretty girl too. But no one will marry her without a dowry, and we don't have a single ruble saved up for her. What does your Talmud tell you about this?

REBBE: This is indeed a complication. I must think.

DEVOREH: Well, eat while you think, Dear. Our soup is getting cold.

The REBBE leads DEVORAH in a brief blessing.

REBBE and DEVORAH: Barukh ata Adonai Eloheinu melekh ha'olam hamotzi lehem min ha'aretz.

They begin eating, then freeze. DEVORAH holds her spoon. The REBBE holds his spoon close to his mouth. Then they unfreeze.

REBBE: Devoreh, I have an answer. We allow rich men to disburden themselves of their great wealth. If a rich man gives money to 100 poor men, the rich man is much better off, and not one of the poor men will receive so much money as to make them rich. The poor remain happily poor but perhaps will not experience the deprivations you have pointed out to me. We solve everyone's problems. The rich and the poor will be delighted by this plan.

DEVOREH: This may be a good plan. I don't know. Where will we find a rich Jew?

REBBE: In Vilna. I will travel to Vilna. There must be many rich Jews there who suffer terribly from their wealth. They will be overjoyed when I explain my plan. Surely there are many poor Jewish villages in the Eastern lands, enough for every rich Jew. I need only get things started. After a while, people will see how well my plan works, and others will adopt it. I will start with Yaakov Kovner. He is a banker and the richest Jew in Vilna. I will set out in two days. I will speak to Ezra and Shaul. They often travel to Vilna to sell their goods. They will tell me everything I need to know about Vilna.

[Scene 2]

> YAAKOV KOVNER is talking in his richly appointed study to his son, MOSHE, who stands before him respectfully.

MOSHE: I am so sorry, father. I tried very hard to do well at the bank. But Mr. Kolitz told me not to return.

YAAKOV: He works for me. I can overrule him if I want. But, ultimately there is no benefit in this. You are a good boy, Moishe, but you are not well suited for business like your brothers are. It is too bad that you do not have a bent toward scholarship. You have the heart and soul of a rabbi.

MOSHE: Yes, I think I would enjoy the life of a rabbi, but that is not to be. Father, do you know what I would like to do?

YAAKOV: *(Brightening.)* Tell me, my Son!

MOSHE: I would like to bake bread. I like the smell of the flour and the smell of the warm bread when it comes from the oven. I like the idea of working hard to make something that people really need. I would give away much of my bread.

YAAKOV: Alas. We cannot pursue this idea. You will never lack for anything in this world, but it would shame our family if you were to go to work as a baker.

MOSHE: I understand.

> MOSHE prepares to leave.

YAAKOV: You are a good boy, Moishe.

MOSHE: Thank you, Father.

> MOSHE exits. YAAKOV stands and puts the back of his hand to his forehead in a gesture of frustration or despair. MOSHE knocks and after a moment re-enters.

MOSHE: Father, Hyam says there is a man at the door who wants to speak to you. Hyam says he is badly dressed. He says he is the rabbi of Pumpian.

YAAKOV: I have heard of that place. Tell Hyam to bring him up to see me. Tell him to prepare tea . . . Tea and kugel. The man may be hungry.

[Scene 3]

> YAAKOV and REBBE NACHMAN are seated around a small table. They drink tea. REBBE NACHMAN eats the kugel heartily. YAAKOV only nibbles. Throughout the scene there is an air of bemusement in YAAKOV'S manner. He respects the rabbi for his good intentions and deep study of sacred texts, but he judges, rightly, that he is a very naïve man.

YAAKOV: There is much to what you say about the burdens of being rich. I do not think, however, that God always chooses to punish men who have become rich. This depends on how they became rich and how they live their lives.

REBBE: Surely, you are right. But, setting aside the question of God's punishment, being rich is a great and terrible burden. I have read this in several holy books.

YAAKOV: *(With bemused irony.)* Yes. Yes. And I thank you for choosing me to be the first rich Jew that you will help. And perhaps we should put your plan to work. Tell me, Rebbe Nachman. About how many families are there in Pumpian?

REBBE: There are different ways to determine what is a family. In some cases the people who live under one roof might be regarded as two families. But I would say there are about 40 families in Pumpian.

YAAKOV: It is indeed a small village. And, about how much money do you think families in Pumpian earn in a year . . . I know, this varies from family to family. But if you were to name one amount of money that is right in the middle, what would that be?

REBBE: Mr. Kovner. This is hard to know exactly. Perhaps a man works, with the help of a strong son, as a blacksmith. That will be a wealthy man. But in another family, only the man works. Perhaps they have four young children. Perhaps this man works in a stable. This situation is very different. But, putting everything together, maybe the middle figure is 200 rubles for each family in a year.

YAAKOV: Just 200 rubles! This is indeed a poor village . . . Rebbe Nachman, I think we are friends now. May I ask how much money *you* earn in a year.

REBBE: This is no secret. The congregation pays me 100 rubles each year. They can do no better. Also, I get a few kopeks when I marry a couple or when I preside over a funeral. And my wife, Devoreh, she knits shawls that are sold in Vilna. So, in a year we take in perhaps 150 rubles.

YAAKOV: Rebbe, how well can you live on 150 rubles a year?

REBBE: Not so well, but well enough. Devoreh keeps a garden. We live simply. But . . .

YAAKOV: But?

REBBE: If, God forbid, severe illness were to come to our door, and we needed medicine from Vilna, we might not be able to afford the medicine. Also, our daughter Rebecca. She is ready to marry. But we have no money for a dowry.

YAAKOV: But she is the daughter of a rabbi.

REBBE: This makes no difference in Pumpian.

YAAKOV: I see. That is too bad. Rebbe Nachman. *(Again with bemused irony.)* You have made me very aware of how much I suffer being rich. I welcome this opportunity to disburden myself of some of my wealth. And it is always good to do a mitzvah . . . I would be pleased to give each family in Pumpian 50 rubles each year. With this money, they could live better— pay for medicine. But if a family goes from, say, 200 to 250 rubles each year, they are still poor—yes? They are in no danger of becoming miserable from their wealth. Is that not so?

REBBE: Yes, I agree with you. However, I am not so good with finances. Tell me. Is this 50 rubles that you propose to give each year to the families of Pumpian enough money to bring down the level of *your* wealth to the point where *you* will no longer be miserable?

YAAKOV: *(Smiling to himself.)* It will be a good start. And there are so many other poor Jewish villages I can give money to. Perhaps I can find other rich Jews who want to relieve their misery as I am doing. We will have to see about that.

REBBE: Yes, perhaps we should start small with my plan. Let people see, as an example, the mutual benefit to both you and the people of Pumpian. Then, the idea will catch fire across all Jewish Russia.

YAAKOV: Yes, that may be. *(Pause.)* I think it is better to give out the money on a monthly basis. Poor people become dazzled and confused when too much money comes to them at once. I propose 5 rubles per family each month. I will need a trustworthy man to distribute the money. So, Rebbe Nachman, that would be you. Also, I predict that sometimes there will be disputes. The people living under one roof will declare themselves to be two separate families and will want two allotments of money. Perhaps they are right and perhaps not. Who better to decide these things than the village rabbi?

REBBE: Oh, no. Mr. Kovner. I cannot do such a thing. I have many duties to perform as rabbi. Also, while I can interpret Jewish law for the community and resolve certain differences of opinion, I am not so good about keeping accounts, keeping track of who has and has not gotten their money. Perhaps one family was visiting relatives in another village when I came around with their rubles, and so I miss them. Then, I must remember to give them two payments when they return.

YAAKOV: Yes, I did not think of the difficulties you would face giving out the money. Perhaps there should be some extra fee for you in return for the extra work.

REBBE: Oh, no. Mr. Kovner. I would never accept a fee for distributing money that you are giving to our village. I simply cannot do this job.

YAAKOV: Your wife, then—Devoreh. Can she read and write, keep records?

REBBE: Surely, she can. But the people of Pumpian would be deeply upset if a woman gave them money and settled their disputes. It can only be a man.

 YAAKOV thinks hard and abstractedly stands.

YAAKOV: Tell me about your daughter. "Rebecca," you said. How old is she? Is she gentle or a shrew? Can she read and write?

REBBE: She is a lovely girl, 19 years of age. Pretty and very smart. Devoreh and I have taught her much more than the very little they teach girls in our school. Rebecca reads and writes Hebrew and Russian, as well as Yiddish. She can read Polish and some German. She can sing. She is religious and dutiful. She has a loving heart.

YAAKOV: Indeed, she is a treasure. Let me tell you about my son, Moshe. He is a good boy. Not so good in business, but good enough for any business you have in Pumpian. Certainly good enough to distribute rubles each month. Perhaps we can arrange a match between my Moshe and your Rebecca. If the couple agrees, of course. Moshe is a handsome boy. A kindly boy. You say Rebecca has a loving heart. So does Moshe. And you said that Rebecca is interested in marriage?

REBBE: Yes, she is. This might make a very good match. But, would Moshe want to live in our little village? And, I have no dowry. Surely in Vilna the father of the groom expects a large dowry.

YAAKOV: I think Moshe would be happy in your village. Life moves at a slow pace there, and I think that would be good for him. And, he can easily visit his mother and me in Vilna. The trip is just a day's journey by coach or wagon. The dowry? My dear Rebbe. Your gift. Your plan by which I am relieving my misery. This is a fine dowry.

REBBE: Yes, I think it is. This is very good. Rebecca has lived in Pumpian all her life. She knows every family. She is shrewd and thoughtful—but always fair-minded in her opinions. If there are disputes or problems in giving out the rubles, Rebecca can advise Moshe privately. Of course, they have not even met. But I am very hopeful.

YAAKOV is visibly struck by a new and exciting idea.

YAAKOV: Moshe has his heart set on a humble occupation: baking bread. And a man should work at something. A son of Yaakov Kovner could not possibly be seen baking bread in Vilna. But in Pumpian . . . Could Moshe bake bread in Pumpian?

REBBE: Yes, this would be very possible. Shmuel, our baker, is old and has no children. I think he and his wife would be very pleased if Moshe were to join the business and, in due time, take it over.

YAAKOV: I think God has led you to my door! Let me invite Moshe to join us. I'd like you to meet him so you can give a report to Rebecca. He is handsome. You'll see. He is well mannered, kind. *(With growing enthusiasm.)* Pious, and a good boy. I promise you. I will call him in. He will be surprised, but very pleased.

YAAKOV and the REBBE stand but do not face the audience for applause. MOSHE enters escorted by DEVOREH. REBECCA enters from the other side of the stage. MOSHE and REBECCA, standing downstage, beam at each other in delight. YAAVOV produces a bottle of vodka and pours three glasses. DEVOREH, MOSHE, and YAAKOVE gather, lift their glasses, and call out, "L'chaim!" MOSHE and REBECCA kiss.

The End

Postscript to "The Rabbi and the Banker"

Reuben Asher Braudes was primarily a Zionist activist and journalist, not a fiction writer. I am not especially fond of his short story, except for the intriguing idea with which it begins: The rabbi, studying holy texts, comes to believe that rich men are made miserable by their wealth and would welcome being disburdened of their riches. Braudes mocks the rabbi as a naïve fool. Braudes' rabbi is also greedy. He wants poor scholars such as himself to be first in line to when all this money is being given away. I believe that Braudes is making the point that social change cannot be achieved by naïve men. His story ends with the rich Jew—the source of his wealth is not stated—essentially tricking the rabbi, "Let us work together! You shall persuade the rich to give away their misfortune, and I will persuade the poor to take it! Your share of the work will be easier. Do your part, and as soon as you have finished with the rich, I will arrange for you to be met half-way by the poor . . ." Through this means, the rich Jew rids himself of his annoying visitor.

I took the Braudes' idea in a different direction, and I added Rebecca and Moshe to the story. Yaakov Kovner, my rich Jew, is generous. He's willing to take upon himself the minor financial burden of easing the lives of the poor Jews of Pumpian. He may laugh to himself at Rebbe Nachman's naivety, but he respects the rabbi because the rabbi's idea comes from his study of holy texts and because Rebbe Nachman (in the play) is in no way seeking personal gain. We ourselves can appreciate Rebbe Nachman's conviction that everyone benefits when wealth is shared, rather than stored up by a few rich people. The happy irony is that Rebbe Nachman's impractical vision is fulfilled, at least for the people of Pumpian.

After Kovner has decided to alleviate the poverty in Pumpian, he realizes that he may have solved his own pressing problem: What to do about Moshe, his unworldly son. It is fun to see Kovner, who has been subtly condescending toward Rebbe Nachman, cozy up to him in his eagerness to arrange his son's match with Rebecca. Also, because all the characters are admirable, we relish the play's happy ending.

It is unfortunate and bothersome that the play, following the outline of Braudes' story, reflects the sexism of the 19th century. But at least I was able to make the play's two women, Devoreh and Rebecca, much more perceptive than the men, Rebbe Nachman and Moshe Kovner, that they are paired with.

Nationalities

A 10-minute play by

David K. Farkas

Setting:

New York City, Sometime in the 1930s, in the midst of the Great Depression.

Characters:

Joe Geller: A smart, ambitious Jew, just out of accounting school.
Sammy D.: The head of a Mafia family in New York City.
Dominic: Joe's friend from baseball and Sammy D's nephew.

[Scene 1]

Offstage voices of JOE and DOMINIC. They enter wearing casual street clothes. DOMINIC has a lot of extra energy.

JOE: Hey Dom. Still throwing that slider?

DOMINIC: Yeah, with the fast ball. And the change-up.

JOE: No one could hit that slider.

DOMINIC: Well, we won a few. *(Laughingly, he gives up the false modesty.)*

DOMINIC pitches a ball in pantomime.

DOMINIC: Hell, we won more than a few!

DOMINIC turns serious.

DOMINIC: Joe, You got a job yet?

JOE: No. Not yet.

DOMINIC: I guess it's tough times.

JOE: Yeah. Not many ads in the help wanteds, and salaries are sure low. But I'll find something.

DOMINIC: You did finish accountant school?

JOE: Yeah, Sure.

DOMINIC: What about going to work for my Uncle Sammy?

JOE: Sammy D.? I always figured on working for a Jewish business. And the stuff Sammy does ain't exactly kosher.

DOMINIC: Sammy's little businesses ain't much worse than what big corporations do. It's just harder for the little guy to get by because up in Albany, they don't write laws to help *us*. Anyways, Uncle Sammy's been saying he could use a smart accountant. I told him I'd ask you. He'd pay real well, I can tell you that.

JOE: Sammy D. wants to hire me?

DOMINIC: Yeah. Italians are comfortable with Jews. We especially like Jewish doctors, Jewish accountants . . . Jewish mechanics, plumbers—not so much.

JOE: There's a Jewish carpenter you liked pretty well.

DOMINIC: Yeah, something like that. But that was a thousand years ago. These days, your Jewish carpenters don't cut so straight. *(Mimics bad sawing.)* and don't hit the nails so even. *(Mimics bad hammering.)*. We'll take our own people for carpentry and plumbing. Hell, we'll take Polacks. *(Laughing.)* We'll take anybody. *(Long pause.)* My Uncle Sammy —he's an OK guy. And, if you're loyal to him, he's loyal to you.

JOE: I'll go talk to him.

DOMINIC: *(Voice fading as they exit.)* Yeah.

JOE: Yea, Thanks, Dom. *(Fading to silence.)* I think I'm gonna . . .

They exit.

[Scene 2]

SAMMY sits at a big desk with a cigar box and a cigar-sized ash tray. JOE, now wearing a sport jacket, is standing in front of the desk.

JOE: So the total from the Brooklyn betting parlors is 930. That's up 10% from last quarter.

SAMMY: That's a good number, Joe. I don't think anyone's holding out on us . . . In maybe six months we'll ask for more money, but not yet . . . Anything else to take care of?

JOE: Just one more thing, Mr. D. Still no payment from Guardino.

SAMMY: Is that right? I'll send some guys to visit him. He'll pay up quick.

JOE exits. SAMMY does some desk work in preparation Scene 4.

[Scene 3]

JOE and DOMINIC are standing downstage.

DOMINIC: I hear it's going well for you. I hear Uncle Sammy likes you.

JOE: I think so, Dom.

DOMINIC: I got stuff going too. Big stuff. When I come strolling down Baxter Street, people gonna notice me. The guys, they'll tip their hats.

[Scene 4]

SAMMY sits at his desk. JOE stands in front of the desk.

JOE: Still no payment from Guardino.

SAMMY: Joe, don't worry about it.

JOE: Should I send another letter?

SAMMY: Joe, I said don't worry about it. Just clear the books on that account. Mark it, "All debts paid in full."

JOE is a bit startled when he grasps what SAMMY has communicated. Then JOE looks at the audience and does a comic double-take to share the ideas that Guardino has been killed.

[Scene 5]

SAMMY D. and DOMINIC are standing.

SAMMY: Joe, I'm gonna ask you to do something special—out of your usual line of work. You can say no . . . There's some risk here.

JOE: Is it important to you?

SAMMY: Yes. Some of my guys broke a rule. And it was with the Luchese Family. That's real stupid. They are the worst people to start trouble with. I want to negotiate with Marco Luchese. Get ourselves out of this. I apologized on the phone to Marco. He listened, but that's not close to enough. He's lost money . . . and, much more than that, he's *offended*.

JOE: A bad situation. How can I help?

SAMMY: We'd like you to meet with Marco and his guys. Handle the negotiations on our side.

JOE: OK. I'll do it. But why me?

SAMMY: Well, you're smart. And, maybe even more important for this situation . . . you're sort of a neutral party. Not in the family. Just an employee. That adds a little distance. Makes the meeting less emotional than if he's looking straight at one of us.

JOE: OK.

SAMMY: Marco's not the calm type. Most guys get to head families because they're smart—and that usually means calm, careful. Marco, he's smart but he's not calm. He's a very emotional guy. So you're a good choice to meet with Marco. No history. No close involvement. Also, they know *you* won't try any funny stuff. That reduces the tension . . .

JOE: You've been real good to me, Mr. D. I'll take on anything to get you out of a jam.

SAMMY: Thank you, Joe. No matter how the meeting goes, I don't think they'll hurt you.

JOE: *(Smiling.)* That's good to know—especially when you tell me Marco's a hothead.

SAMMY: I think you'll be OK. Killing our Jewish accountant? Wouldn't prove a thing. When the families found out, he'd just get laughed at. "So, Marco, he gets mad at Sammy D. And you know what he does? He offs Sammy's little Jewish accountant!" "What! He did *that?*" *(SAMMY fakes the derisive laughter he's imagining.)*

JOE: Thanks a lot.

SAMMY: You know what I mean.

JOE: What if they grab me and make me give up stuff I know? The accounts. The payoffs.

SAMMY: Joe, you're always thinking. We like that. But that's how a Jewish accountant thinks. Not us. There's nothing to worry about on that score. That's just not what we do. I'm 90% certain they won't kill you. I'm 80% certain they won't rough you up. But I'm 100% sure they won't try to squeeze information out of you.

JOE: When do you want me to go?

SAMMY: Tomorrow.

JOE: Mr. D.—tomorrow's Yom Kippur.

SAMMY: I know that. The meeting is at 4:00. It will be over with enough time for you to get to shul before sundown. You're allowed to work right up until sundown. Right?

SAMMY: We don't need to hear from you until after Yom Kippur. Whatever happens at your meeting, just go straight from the meeting to shul. Come back to work on Thursday.

JOE: OK. If that's how you want it.

SAMMY: Here's the deal. As a peace offering, tell Marco he can have our numbers game south of Mott Street. That's a big area. That's giving up a lot. And . . . I'll sign over the deed to our plot in the new addition to Green-Wood Cemetery. It's beautiful and big enough for 20 graves. It's up on a little hill with a view of the City. Almost as nice as the Pierrepont Family plot nearby. That's offering Marco a lot. That's respectability. Maybe he'll ask for something else. I don't know. Just use your head. Be real flexible here. We don't want a war. They are bigger than us. *(Long pause and then a serious tone of voice.)* One thing: What we really don't want to give up is the warehouse on 12th Street.

JOE: *(A little suspiciously.)* OK, the warehouse on 12th Street.

SAMMY: It's gonna be part of the conversation, but try like hell not to give that up. But do it up if it means preventing a war. And, Joe. You Jews. On Yom Kippur you got a prayer to keep people in the Book of Life? Big part of the service. Yes?

JOE: Yeah that's right.

SAMMY: Well, do some praying for . . . people you know, our people. Pray to God to keep our people safe.

JOE: That's not exactly what Yom Kippur prayer is about.

SAMMY: Joe, just do it. I'm asking.

JOE: I'll do it. I'll do everything you're asking me.

[Scene 6]

SAMMY is at his desk, on which there is now a whiskey bottle and a glass. JOE is standing.

JOE: Mr. D.

SAMMY: Yeah, Joe.

JOE: I had to give up the warehouse. You were right. That's what Marco wanted. I couldn't get him off that. I tried.

No reaction from SAMMY D.

JOE: But there's not gonna be a war. Isn't that what counts?

SAMMY: Yeah, Joe.

JOE: You don't seem happy, Mr. D. It's just a *warehouse*. And none of what I'm saying seems like news to you.

SAMMY: It's not news, Joe. We know about your meeting. I talked to Marco yesterday while you were at shul. We met face to face at the place he likes to go for lunch. I took a little chance there.

JOE: Mr. D. What could be so important about that warehouse? I know that street end to end. There's not one special building on that street.

SAMMY: The warehouse is a person, Joe. One of the guys who offended Marco. You gave Marco an authorized hit on someone.

JOE: Who? Which person?

SAMMY: You don't need to know.

JOE: Yes I do. Tell me, Mr. D. Please.

SAMMY: It's Dominic. The "warehouse" stood for Dominic. Dom's one of the guys who offended, and the one who should have known better. Dom thought he was gonna show Marco what a tough guy he is, how smart he is. Didn't tell me anything about his big idea. Well, he wasn't so smart, and of the three, Dom's the guy Marco picked out for retribution. Dom offended Marco badly. Undermined his reputation. Now Marco needs to assert himself, show he's the big guy. That's how it works here.

JOE: No, not Dominic!

SAMMY: I tried to save him. I begged. I *begged*. I offered everything.

JOE: Not Dominic!

SAMMY: Dom brought it on himself. It was either Dominic's dead or else a couple of Dominics are dead. And some of their Dominics besides. No one knows where it would have stopped.

JOE: You should have told me before I met with Marco.

SAMMY: No, it was better you didn't know what you were offering up. You wouldn't have been calm if you knew you were talking about Dom.

JOE: Where's Dominic now?

SAMMY: No one knows just where he is. We don't want to know. He's cut off now. And if you try to help Dom, Marco will likely find out. Don't do it, Joe. Don't be a fool. In your Jewish world of tailors and barbers, you can get through life being a fool. But in my world, the families from Italy and Sicily, young fools like Dominic don't last long.

JOE: Mr. D., I may be able to fix this.

SAMMY: You?

JOE: Yes. The world's divided up in lots of ways. There's Irish, Italians, and Jews, There's union guys and rich guys. There's smart and dumb. There's old and young. Dom and me, we're both young guys. We know things you and Marco don't.

SAMMY: What are you saying?

JOE: Dominic is seeing Theresa Luchese, seeing her a lot, more than "seeing" her—they have plans.

SAMMY: You know this?

JOE: Yes. And I know more. The young men and women, we have our allies. The mothers and the aunts and the grandmothers who care more about weddings and children than about business and family honor . . . If Marco has Dominic killed, he'll be dealing with all the womenfolk around him. They'll be "offended" much worse than Dominic offended Marco. Marco will wish he had the plot in Green-Wood Cemetery so he could dig himself a hole, jump in, and escape from his daughter.

SAMMY: OK. OK. Let's go visit Luchese. I think the terms of the deal are different now . . . But if you're lying to save your friend, you've stopped being a smart Jew on his way up. You'll be just one more of those reckless young fools who don't live long. Now tell me one more time. Is Dominic really with Theresa Luchese? Do they plan to get married?

JOE: I'm no liar! You know that. Dom and Theresa Luchese are as deep in love as you can get. Marco is going to have to accept that. Dom didn't tell me about his stupid stunt to impress the man who'll be his father-in-law. If I'd known, I would have stopped it.

SAMMY: OK. Other than this recent thing, Marco never had anything against Dom. I'm gonna hate to give up the numbers business south of Mott Street, and I'll really hate to give up the plots at Green-Wood . . . My God! One day Dominic could be buried there with Theresa . . .

JOE: There's a thought. Right there next to the Pierrepont family. Dom's moving up in the world.

SAMMY: Yeah, but he owes me *big*. And, if he ever gets to serious fighting with Theresa, she'll remind him that she's the reason he's even alive. But, this is a pretty good day . . . for everyone. Joe, I like your praying. I like your shul. Looks like we're all in that Book of Life.

The End

Postscript to "Nationalities"

My Uncle Joe was a savvy, rough-edged Jewish accountant who would cut corners in the interest of his clients. He had more than his share of clients who had cut a few corners of their own and were looking at big trouble from the IRS. Joe was short and stocky. He talked fast and loud and punctuated his sentences with a poke from his ever-present cigar. He was funny and irreverent—great fun at family gatherings. I wrote this play while visiting relatives in and around New York City. Among them were Uncle Joe's daughter, daughter-in-law, grandchildren, and great grandchildren. Joe was much on my mind during the trip.

Just as in "Nationalities," Joe's first job after accounting school was working for the head of a Mafia family. They liked Joe, but—in contrast to the Joe Geller of the play—my Uncle Joe chose to leave. As he learned more about the family's businesses, he decided that, regardless of the pay, this was not what he wanted to be doing. When he told his boss he was quitting, this was the response: "Joe, we hate to lose you, but it's a good thing you decided now. Another six months, and there would be no getting out." Beyond the circumstance that my uncle started his accounting career working for a Mafia family, the play is entirely fiction.

In the play, Joe shows himself to be smart, honest, brave, and loyal. Sammy D. is judicious and, within the limits of his Mafia code and culture, honorable and humane. But the real heroes are the "mothers and the aunts and the grandmothers who care more about weddings and children than about business and family honor." Marco Luchese has good reason to fear his daughter's fury if he has Dominic killed. Female values triumph.

Jews and Italians

"Nationalities" reflects my childhood experience that Jews and Italians are very compatible. The Rolling Hills subdivision in Clifton, NJ, where we lived, was about 40% Jewish and about 50% Roman Catholic, mostly Italians but some Poles and other Eastern European Catholics. Protestants mostly chose not to live in our neighborhood. The Jews and Italians got along great. They went to our bar mitzvahs. (We had no bat mitzvahs back then.) We celebrated Christmas and Easter at their homes. I enjoyed some wonderful dinners in which the tomato sauce had been a bushel basket full of fresh tomatoes that morning. The boys in the neighborhood would shout "kike" and "wop" back and forth, but no one took offense. From my experience, there is nothing surprising or implausible about Sammy D.'s familiarity with Yom Kippur and his solemn request that Joe "do a little praying for our people."

There were some intriguing differences between the Jews and the Italians. The predominant design of the cookie-cutter homes comprising our subdivision included a portico with columns of wrought-iron grill work. The Jews opted for relatively plain columns. Italian families opted for elaborate grill work. A family named Grilli had so much wrought iron grill work that their home seemed to be a pun on the family name.

Many of the homes had partial façades made of stone. The Jewish families, including ours, chose bland tan and gray stone (or no façade at all). The Italians almost always chose colorful marble. The developer of the subdivision, a Mr. Kramer, himself a Jew, knew just what decorative options to offer his customers. The Italians seemed to be re-creating, in America, some grand estate in their ancestral Italian town. The Jews seemed to think it was safer not to live in a showy house that might make their Gentile neighbors envious. Another difference: Several Italian families regularly left empty 5-liter Gallo wine jugs next to their garbage cans. The Jews were not wine drinkers, but if they were, they'd never set out empty wine jugs for all the world to see.

When Dominic jokes that Italians seek out Jewish accountants and doctors but steer clear of Jewish mechanics and plumbers, he is echoing what was, at least in that time, a familiar and largely accurate stereotype about Jews. They were largely apartment dwellers who would always call the "super" when something went wrong with a faucet or a window shade. They never worked on their cars. In Rolling Hills, the Jews were unlikely to have a workbench and set of power tools in their garage.

Regional Distributor

A 10-minute play by

David K. Farkas

Setting:

The small showroom of Main Street Quality Furniture, in Utica, New York, during the Great Depression. The store has become the much larger Main Street Appliance in 1947.

Characters:

Al Farkas: A young sales rep for Colony Furniture, a New Jersey manufacturer of inexpensive bedroom sets.

Al Farkas' Doppelgänger: Invisible to everyone, but he can speak privately to Al. "Al" pivots to become the Doppelgänger.

Abe Goldberg: The owner of a struggling furniture store in Utica, New York.

Stewart: Abe's son.

Mr. Atkinson: The New York State Sales Manager for the Frigidaire Company.

Narrator

Suggested casting:

Al Farkas/Al's doppelgänger
Abe
Narrator/Mr. Atkinson/Stewart

[Scene 1]

> The scene is the interior of the small, run-down furniture store. ABE
> GOLDBERG, the owner, is lounging on one of two light-colored
> upholstered chairs, part of a living room set. He is smoking a cigar and
> looking bored. The NARRATOR enters.

NARRATOR: It is 1936, in the depths of the Great Depression. Al Farkas, a
young, energetic furniture salesman, has just stepped into Main Street
Quality Furniture, in Utica, New York. He is paying a sales call on the
owner, Abe Goldberg. Al represents the Colony Furniture Company, in
Linden, New Jersey. His territory is New York State and Northern New
Jersey.

> The NARRATOR exits. AL, carrying a thick sample book, enters with big
> strides.

AL: Hiya, Abe.

ABE: Come on in, Al.

AL: Good to see you. Ya sellin' any furniture these days? *(Chuckles.)* No
one else is.

> ABE stands up to meet AL and shakes his hand warmly. ABE is
> unimpressively dressed in a casual shirt and slacks.

ABE: I figured it was about time for you to be stoppin' by. Where did you
come here from?

DOPPEL: Gee, this place looks awful. I wonder if Abe will hang on much
longer.

AL: Buffalo, Rochester, Syracuse. From here, it's Albany and then home.
Been out a week.

> With his cigar fully noticeable, ABE sits himself back in the upholstered
> chair and gestures for AL to sit in the matching chair.

ABE: Well, take a load off.

DOPPEL: My God, he sits there with his lit cigar in a chair he's trying to
sell to customers.

AL: Sure, Abe.

ABE: Ya wanna drink?

AL: No, I'm OK. But thanks.

ABE pulls out a whiskey bottle and a shot glass that were tucked between the upholstered chair and a table lamp. He pours himself a drink and does not return the bottle.

DOPPEL: *(Ironically.)* This will look great if a customer comes in! But Abe's pretty safe on that score.

AL: How's Marge?

ABE: Marge is doing a lot better. The doctor is encouraging now.

AL: That's good, Abe. On top of business being lousy, you sure don't need to be worrying about Marge. What about the boys?

ABE: They're doing great. Good in school. Good on the sports teams. Just real good.

AL: Well, that's terrific.

ABE nods.

AL: What's that Frigidaire doin' over there?

ABE: Long story. Hey, Al. I sold two of your dark maple bedroom sets last month.

AL: Hey, that's *good.* We got a new smoky maple now. *(Opens sample book.)* We never did a finish like before.

AL shows ABE a page from the sample book.

ABE: You like it?

AL: I don't know. If it sells, I'll like it. Maybe I'll ship you one dark maple and one smoky maple. See what happens.

ABE: Sure. You know what? I'll take a medium maple too. You know, the regular one.

DOPPEL: Maybe I should give him a discount. If I throw in the second night table, I'll probably take a dollar cut on my commission for each of the bedroom sets. What the hell.

AL: OK, with an order of three bedroom sets, I think we can throw in the second night table for free.

ABE: That's great. Thanks. Customers like that second night table. Can I count on that? Ongoing?

AL: Yeah, if you phone or mail in any order of three or more bedroom sets, we'll give you the second night table. I'll tell the girls in the office.

ABE: OK! OK!

AL: So what's with the Frigidaire? You trying to sell refrigerators?

DOPPEL: What's Abe thinking? Who's gonna come in here to buy a Frigidaire? I don't even think it's plugged in. If a customer was interested in a refrigerator, wouldn't they want to feel inside?

ABE: Well, six weeks ago this fella walks in. A goy. Well-dressed. Sure not a customer.

> ATKINSON enters and stands at the periphery, isolated and unaware. ABE stands out of respect for his visitor. He is facing ATKINSON, although he is clearly addressing AL.

ABE: He tells me he's the New York State sales manager for Frigidaire. Mr. Walter Atkinson, based in Manhattan. He says he needs a regional distributor for Oneida County. He says there's not a lot of businesses around here selling durables. He sure got that right! Would I like to be the regional distributor for Frigidaire? He says ice boxes are a thing of the past. I say, "This is a *furniture* store."

> ATKINSON "comes to life," steps forward, and picks up the dialog with ABE. AL just observes.

MR. ATKINSON: Yes, it's a furniture store, Mr. Goldberg. But that's OK. You don't really need to have customers come *in here* and buy Frigidaires. You get a commission whether the customer comes in or not. To become our regional distributor, you have to have one unit in your store. That's the requirement.

ABE: A Frigidaire is pretty *big*—huh. I think it would confuse my customers. When they come in they won't know if it's a furniture store or what.

MR. ATKINSON: Well, it doesn't need to be in any special location. You can put it anywhere in the store.

DOPPEL: *(Breaking in.)* This is one strange story.

ABE: What's it gonna cost me?

MR. ATKINSON: Thirty-five dollars. That's the wholesale price, of course. We cover shipping.

ABE: Mr. Atkinson, that's a lot of money. These are hard times. I can't take that kind of money out of the business.

MR. ATKINSON: *(Looking at his watch.)* I understand. How about this? We'll ship the unit, and you can pay for it out of your commissions.

ABE: Really? Well, I don't see how I can lose on that deal.

MR. ATKINSON: No, I don't see how you can . . . OK, so we'll sign some papers, and my work here is done.

After a pause, ATKINSON exits.

ABE: Well, that's it. No one has come in to look at a Frigidaire. Most of my customers don't even ask about it. Maybe they don't see it there. A few walk over and take a look. No reason to waste money on electricity, so I keep it shut down.

AL stands, getting ready to leave.

AL: That's quite a story. *(Chuckling.)* Well, I got a few more calls to make this afternoon. *(Laughing.)* Hey, Abe, if you plugged it in, you could keep your sandwiches and cola nice and cold . . . Well, good luck to you and your Frigidaire. And good luck with the smoky maple.

AL exits.

[Scene 2]

ABE is lounging on what looks like the same chair and is smoking a cigar. The NARRATOR enters.

NARRATOR: Al is making another sales call on Abe Goldberg. It's about one year since the day he saw the Frigidaire in Abe's store.

The NARRATOR exits. AL, carrying a thick sample book, steps inside.

AL: Hiya, Abe. How'ya doin'. Ya sellin' any furniture these days?

ABE: Al, nice to see you!

ABE stands for a warm handshake.

ABE: You should come by more often.

AL: I'll try to, but I do most of my business now in New Jersey and Brooklyn.

DOPPLE: Abe's lookin' healthy. The store isn't any better.

ABE: Well, take a load off.

AL: Sure.

ABE sits himself back in the same chair and gestures for AL to sit in the matching chair. He sits.

AL: So what's goin' on?

ABE: Al, I can't give you no business. Nothing's moved off the floor in two weeks.

AL: That's OK. I get some orders. We shipped *you* three smoky maples two months back.

ABE: Johnson Brothers, in Franklin, closed three weeks ago. Some of their business might come to me, but it won't be much. They were not my favorite people, but—still—it's sad to see another business go under.

DOPPLE: Well, there's that Frigidaire. Whatya know, it's plugged in. I guess Abe is keeping his sandwiches cold.

AL: *(Laughing.)* How's the Frigidaire?

ABE: It's a *new* model. Take a close look. *(Points.)* A truck brought it in here and took out the other one. You know, I'm making some money on that thing. People come in here now specially to look at my Frigidaire. A few buy, most don't. I'm not the only store in the area selling refrigerators. But, I'm still the regional distributor for the Frigidaire Corporation, and whenever a Frigidaire sells anywhere in Oneida County, I get a cut. Check from New York City comes every month. Saw Mr. Atkinson just once. He asked if everything was OK. I said it was.

AL: You get checks from New York City. How 'bout that! . . . How's Marge? How's the family?

ABE: They're good. Marge says we should think about a vacation. Maybe go to Miami Beach after New Year's.

ABE and AL trail off into pantomime.

[Scene 3]

The stage is bare. AL enters and freezes. He is not carrying his sample book. The NARRATOR enters.

NARRATOR: Ten years have passed. It's 1947. Al has just stepped through the doors of a much larger and more modern incarnation of Abe's store. This is not a sales call. Abe stopped carrying furniture shortly after the war ended. This will be Al's last trip through New York State. He's about to narrow his sales territory to Brooklyn and northern New Jersey.

The NARRATOR exits.

DOPPLE: Be nice to see Abe again. Wow, some place he has now!

STEWART GOLDBERG, in a sport jacket, enters and greets AL.

STEWART: Good morning, sir. Welcome to Main Street Appliance. How may we help you?

AL: Hi. My name's Al Farkas. I'm an old friend of Abe's. Is he in?

STEWART: Mr. Farkas! I'm Stewart, Abe's son. I don't think we've met, but Abe talks about you. You're from the furniture-store days. Really nice to see you. I'm the store manager now. Let me take you back to see Abe.

STEWART and AL exit. AL throws interested glances all around, suggesting a busy store. As they exit, a desk, a swivel desk chair, and a guest chair are brought in. STEWART leads AL to the entrance to ABE'S office. ABE, as actor, takes a seat at the swivel desk chair.

STEWART: Hey Dad, you have a visitor.

STEWART exits to return to the sales floor. ABE turns his chair to face AL.

ABE: So good to see you, Al!

ABE sets down his cigar and rises to shake hands.

AL: I was driving through from Syracuse. Thought I'd drop by and say hello.

ABE: That's great. Thanks for makin' the time. You know, you're lucky you caught me in. And *I'm* lucky you caught me. I'm actually not here that much. The kid pretty much runs the place.

ABE sits in his swivel chair. AL, taking the cue, takes a seat in the guest chair.

AL: I'm sorry about Artie.

ABE: Yeah, time passes, but the pain doesn't really go away. Toughest on Marge. You can imagine. And it wasn't much before V-J Day. Just three weeks. *You* were in the Pacific, right Al?

AL: Yes, I was . . . Well, this place is hoppin'.

ABE: It is. We got customers in here all day. But a lot of our money comes from new construction. People order their refrigerators through the builder when they're planning out the kitchen. We never even see those folks. We're just the "regional distributor." It can't last forever. But Frigidaire has its way of doing things, and they like to follow it . . . I was lucky. Mr. Atkinson just *walked* in here. But I *did* know how to seize an opportunity.

DOPPLE: *(Looking at ABE.)* I think Opportunity seized *you.*

AL: I guess you did, Abe.

DOPPLE: *(Addressing AL.)* One of the worst businessmen you ever sold to! Sometimes lucky is better than smart. But he's a good guy, and Stewart seems like a real nice kid. And hep, too.

ABE: Atkinson actually retired. There's a new guy. I think he's come in twice.

AL: Stewart, he's a real nice boy. That's a blessing. You know that.

ABE: Yeah, Al. That's a blessing.

AL: Abe, I'm married. About a year. I have a son, three months old. I'm gonna give up the travel. I can do plenty of business close to home.

ABE: I'm happy for you. I betcha found a good woman.

AL: Yeah, I think I did. And we're gonna move soon. Down from the Bronx right into Manhattan. Big new housing development—"Stuyvesant Town" they call it. Hard to get in, but I got "veterans' preference."

ABE: Good for you! I think I heard of that place.

AL rises and starts to leave.

AL: Well, I got a few more calls to make this afternoon.

ABE: So nice that you stopped in to see me. It was always really nice when you came in here. More than business. A lot more than business.

AL steps close to ABE, and puts an arm over his shoulder.

AL: That's right. A lot more than business. My best to Marge. Take good care.

ABE: Take good care.

AL exits.

The End

Postscript to "Regional Distributor"

Al told many stories about his experiences in business. The first two scenes of "Regional Distributor" come directly from one of these stories.

My father would laugh as he finished the story, "Sometimes, it's better to be lucky than smart!" The third scene, Al's final visit to Abe's store, is fiction, but the scene does show how Al's life changed after he returned from World War II. It includes his marriage and my birth.

Do you want to know how Abe Goldberg found his way to rural New York State? I may have the answer. Al told me that when a furniture store owner had one or more sons who could take over the business and one son who'd be a detriment, he'd set up the clueless son with a furniture store in some rural town. Without much in the way of competition, the clueless son would not likely go out of business, but he wouldn't get in the way of the "hep" son or sons.

When our informal little theater group staged this play, I could not resist taking the role of Al Farkas. It was a special experience imitating the speaking style of a man I knew so well and, at the end of the play, announcing my own birth .

Jews and "Walters"

Walter Atkinson is a minor but pivotal character. He is just one of the "Walters" in my plays. Walters are my archetypal WASPS (white Anglo-Saxon Protestants). When Abe, an Eastern European Jew, describes Walter Atkinson to Al, another Eastern European Jew, he knows what details matter. Walter Atkinson is a goy, (Abe and Al would assume a Protestant.), he's well dressed, and he's based in Manhattan, meaning that most of the time he works in some impressive office building where Abe and Al would not be welcome. This particular Walter is benign, though condescending toward Abe. But Walters, both in my plays and in real life, were not always benign. I knew a woman whose father spent his entire career working as a chemical engineer for Standard Oil of New Jersey. For fear of being fired by the Walters who ran the company, he never revealed that he was a Jew.

To my father, to Abe, and to many other mid-century American Jews, Walters were the Americans they could never be. Not all Walters were wealthy or powerful, but they were all natural heirs to America, not newcomers, outsiders, forever suspect, if not worse. Once each year Al accompanied Aaron Newman, the owner of the Colony Furniture Company, on a big purchasing trip to High Point, North Carolina. Aaron and Al would examine and negotiate, and Aaron would order railroad cars full of furniture-grade maple and oak. In High Point, Aaron and Al were the customers, and the Walters were looking for the sale. But those Southerners were Walters nevertheless, and Aaron and Al were the Jews. My father envied Walters. He grudgingly respected those who deserved respect, but deep down he bitterly resented all Walters—for a reason I'll now relate.

Before he started with Colony Furniture, Al was a traveling salesman who made lonely six-week sales trips, mostly through Southern states. He sold jewelry, perfume, and other merchandise to Walter store owners. Al was tall, athletic, red-headed, and blue-eyed. His New York City accent was light. Southerners did not take him for a Jew. Not a few times it went down like this: "Sure glad to be buying from you, Al, instead of that damn kike who came through here last week." Al took the orders, but it scarred his soul.

Al's travels through the South ended with World War II. During the war, he passed up the opportunity to have a Walter killed. Al's unit suffered under a very harsh officer. He was hated, for all kinds of reasons, by his men. Late one night, as Al slept in his tent, someone shook and woke him. "Follow me." A kangaroo court was in session. There was at least one person in the unit who was willing to make sure that this officer would not return from the next patrol. The officer hated Jews, and as someone who had been conspicuously mistreated, Al was given a vote. In effect, he was a member of the jury. Al told the story simply, "I thought for a few moments and said, "Don't do it on my account." There weren't enough "guilty" votes, and the men continued to suffer under this guy.

Just like Al, Sammy D. and Marco Luchese, from "Nationalities," know they can never be Walters, but they think that a large family plot in the prestigious Green-Wood cemetery will get them halfway there.

Manny Wolf – Tyrone Young

A 10-minute play by

David K. Farkas

Setting:

A furniture store in a ghetto neighborhood of Newark New Jersey. The play begins just a few weeks before July 12, 1967, the day that a highly destructive race riot broke out in Newark, following an act of unjustified arrest and police brutality. Later, the play moves to a beach area on a part of the South Florida coast favored by Jewish retirees. The play can be performed on a bare stage.

Characters:

MANNY WOLF: An older Jewish man who owns Wolf's Discount Furniture in Newark, NJ.

AL FARKAS: An older Jewish man who, as a manufacturer's rep, pays sales calls on Manny.

TYRONE YOUNG: A young Black man, about 18 years old. Later a successful Black businessman in his early 30s.

SAUL: A Jewish attorney based in Newark.

NARRATOR

Suggested minimum casting:

Manny Wolf
Al Farkas/Saul/Narrator
Tyrone Young

[Scene 1]

NARRATOR: Wolf's Discount Furniture is a Jewish-owned store located on Bergen Avenue in the troubled, largely black Central Ward of Newark, New Jersey. It is the summer of 1967, a time of intense racial tension in cities across the United States. Al Farkas, a sales representative for the Colony Furniture Company, will soon walk through the door to pay a sales call on his customer and friend, Manny Wolf.

> The NARRATOR exits.

MANNY: *(Holding a banker's money pouch.)* Now, Tyrone, be polite, but make it clear that their furniture is going to be repossessed if they don't pay the bill. Everyone on your list is at least two months behind.

TYRONE: OK, Mr. Wolf.

> AL enters carrying his sample book. He approaches MANNY and waits until the conversation with TYRONE is over.

MANNY: And Tyrone, if you meet up with any hoodlum, any kind of stick-up man, or tough guy, just give him the pouch. No hero stuff. OK?

TYRONE: OK, Mr. Wolf.

MANNY: Now, you make your morning run and come right back here with the pouch. Then, I'll give you 5 bucks for lunch. That's on me. Then, after lunch, you go out with a new list for the afternoon run.

TYRONE: OK, Mr. Wolf.

MANNY: Tyrone, I hope you're gonna like working for me.

TYRONE: Yes, Mr. Wolf. It's good to get any work these days.

MANNY: One more thing. I put 100 bucks in the pouch. Fives and tens. Just in case you need to make change. I'll put another 100 in your pouch when you go out again in the afternoon. If I forget, remind me.

TYRONE: OK Mr. Wolf. I won't forget.

MANNY: I don't think you will, Tyrone. Looks like you're a sharp kid.

> TYRONE smiles and exits.

MANNY: Sorry I kept you waiting, Al. I'm glad you stopped in.

AL: No problem. Hey, Manny. Why did you give that kid the 100 dollars in small bills? No one's gonna pay him in big bills. And after the first couple of stops, he should have plenty of small bills, nothing *but* small bills. That's how folks pay around here.

MANNY: Yeah, I know. Al, It's like this. If the kid stays with the job—and that's a big if—he's gonna get robbed. That's for sure. But just in case he's robbed early on his route, before he's collected much dough, I want those guys, those hoodlums, to get at least a 100 bucks. These guys, they're crazy or high on dope. If they don't get any money, they're likely to put a knife into the kid. Or shoot him, right in the hallway of some tenement building. Those guys don't care about nothin'. Police ain't worth shit.

AL: My God. What a crazy situation!

MANNY: Yeah, I hate like hell to lose an extra 100. But, whaddya gonna do? One of the guys that was working for me. He didn't have any money to hand over. They threw him down a stairwell. He's 30 years old, and he's gonna walk with a limp for the rest of his life.

AL: Damn!

MANNY: That's when I started putting the 100 in the pouch. Just the cost of doin' business in the ghetto. Wasn't always like this. When I started, we had lots of Jews in the neighborhood, *and* comin' into the store. Also Italians. Pollocks. Negroes too. No Spanish back then. Anyway, it was a little rough, but nothing like this. We got social breakdown now. Drugs. We got Black Power. They especially hate Jews. I'm glad I don't have many more years before I retire. Goin' down to Florida.

AL: When you figure on closing the store?

MANNY: Maybe five years. Or less, if I just can't stand doin' this anymore. Al, I think you've met Roosevelt—"Rosie"—a few times. He's been my store manager these past three years. No genius, but he's OK. Steady guy, works hard, honest. He's gonna buy the business from me. I'm not asking much either. I got two sons. Neither one will *touch* this place. I don't blame them. Thank God, they have better options.

AL: It's tough, Manny. I'm sorry. But you're sure not the only white guy bailing on Newark. Stores are turning over. More and more Negro owners.

MANNY: Al, did you know I went to college? Got a degree in Business.

AL: No, Manny, you never told me that.

MANNY: Well, I graduated from Fordham, good grades. I'm in Manhattan, interviewing for a job with Metropolitan Life Insurance. Interview is going good. The guy likes me. We've agreed on the salary, everything. So, I say to him, "Mr. Harris"—some name like that—"One more thing, I'll need to take off for the High Holy Days." He says, "You're a Jew? We didn't know you were a Jew. We don't hire Jews here!" They sent me right out the building. That's when I got started in retail, working for another Jew and then for myself. Maybe it's different now, but Jews didn't have the option of working for big corporations in nice office buildings back then. That's why we're in places like this.

AL: Yeah, I understand all about that.

MANNY: Al, I'll tell you the worst part. All this ghetto stuff, crime stuff, no-pay-me stuff. It eats into profits something awful. Just to stay in business I gotta make those losses back. So, a customer comes in here. He's with his wife. Looks respectable, like a church-goer. Maybe he works for the post office. OK, that's good. But a sharpie comes in here. Woman don't look like a wife. He's wearin' . . . you know . . . purple shirt, yellow tie. Hair like Little Richard. So, I say to Rosie, "Now you take good care of these folks." But that's a code for charging them 25% more. Why? The church goers—now they're gonna make their payments. Maybe even pay cash. Little Richard? He's likely to give me trouble. Overdue payments. Or worse. But, here's what I hate. Sometimes, Little Richard, he pays right on time. He turns out to be an upstanding guy, and *I'm* a thief . . . It's time for the schvartzers to take over the businesses in the Central Ward. Let Rosie figure this out. He knows these people better than me. I'm ready for Florida. Five more years, and the wife and I can buy a nice place down there.

AL: I'm sorry you got to deal with all this, Manny. I don't have any answers.

MANNY: Well, let's talk furniture, Al. I'm selling the oak. I'm selling the maple. Folks like that smokey maple of yours. Let's go into my office, where I can look at my sales figures. Then I'll know exactly what I need to order.

They exit.

[Scene 2]

MANNY is standing in his store with a clipboard, some papers, and a pencil. TYRONE bursts in through the door.

TYRONE: Mr. Wolf. There's big trouble. It's all gone crazy up and down Springfield Avenue. There's fires. People breaking into stores. Beatin' people up . . . bad. It's headed down this way. White folks gotta leave. Right now!

MANNY: Do I got time to get money out of the safe?

TYRONE: I guess so. I'll stay outside, maybe try to keep them away from the store. But I'm no Mohammad Ali. I'm just a kid. I don't think I can stop anything.

MANNY: OK, Tyrone. Thanks. Do what you can. Please.

MANNY walks upstage in a hurry, presumably to get to the safe, and exits. (A quick costume change will be necessary.) TYRONE takes short running steps downstage (presumably onto the street). He looks around frantically around him and speaks to himself and to the audience.

TYRONE: There's smoke! They're shootin' guns. It's all coming this way. Oh my God! This is where *we* live. Why we burning *our* part of Newark? Where's the police? . . . Shit! No police gonna stop this.

TYRONE exits running.

[Scene 3]

AL and MANNY, both wearing casual shirts and light-colored, summer-weight slacks, are strolling slowly and intermittently on a street in South Florida. They have big plastic cups and are sipping through straws as they walk.

MANNY: So, you like living in Florida?

AL: Not so much. It's what Sally wanted. But, I'll get used to it.

MANNY: Well, you're in Buena Vista Estates—that's a real nice place.

AL: Yep, no complaints about that.

MANNY: Shirley and I. We're in Grove Hill—not as nice as we'd like. You know, I had to retire early because of the riots.

AL: Yeah, I remember.

MANNY: And of course, the way the insurance guys calculate value, I didn't get squat for the building. Hell, the City of Newark found ways to charge *me* when it all got tore down.

AL: That's rotten. *(Pause.)* I've driven through there, right down on Bergen Street, where you were. It's all a wasteland now. It's pretty much like that on all the business streets in the Central Ward, except that there's some businesses on Springfield.

MANNY: You know the really sad part. It's Rosie. For all its problems, that store made money. Rosie would have had a real business to run. He would have done OK with it too. But there was no opportunity for him when there was no more store. Last I heard, he's standing behind a counter selling chicken wings. I came out with less dough than I expected. But Rosie, he's the one that really got hurt in all this.

AL: I'm sorry 'bout Rosie. I'm sorry about the bad deal you got.

MANNY: They have a Black mayor now. That's a good thing. They have urban renewal plans, even for the Central Ward. Maybe there's hope for the future.

AL: Maybe so. Won't happen soon.

They stroll a little farther.

MANNY: Hey, Al. Well, we're back to our cars. This was a nice walk we took. We gotta get together again. Maybe dinner, with our wives.

AL: Yeah, we need to do that. It was real nice catching up. See you later, Manny.

AL exits, for a quick costume change.

MANNY: *(Thinking aloud and addressing the audience.)* Was I doin' the right thing runnin' that store? Living pretty good off poor people? Raising the price, depending on what someone looked like, how they dressed? After a while, there were much better, much cheaper furniture stores out on the highway. That's where Al was doing most of his business. But those schvartzers, they never thought about driving out there. They shopped right close to where they lived, where everything was familiar. I was half providing a necessary service and half taking advantage. But I was only there because American capitalism. The Big Boys wouldn't hire a Jew. I was left with the dirty end of capitalism, not those nice offices at the Metropolitan Life Insurance Company.

MANNY exits.

[Scene 4: Epilogue]

TYRONE, looking 20 years older, enters. He's flashily dressed in a purple shirt and yellow tie. There is some swagger in his walk. With him and somewhat deferential in manner is SAUL, TYRONE'S real estate attorney.

SAUL: Well, both lots are yours now, Mr. Young. You're gonna have your new building and plenty of parking. Everything is signed. Papers are filed. It's official at the beginning of next month. And a great deal you got.

TYRONE: You did good work, Saul. I plan to use you again.

SAUL: That's terrific. I'm real glad to hear that.

TYRONE: *(Looking at his watch.)* Let's get lunch. Celebrate.

SAUL: Sure.

TYRONE: How about Michaelson's?

SAUL: Yes! Sure.

TYRONE: You know, Saul, I had a job right where my new building is gonna go up. It was a furniture store. The owner was a Jew. I didn't like what I was doing—collecting overdue payments—but I was doing it. The job, though, it lasted only three weeks. Then it ended—kerpoof! And I mean "kerpoof." Never got paid for my last few days.

SAUL: *(Some distress in his voice.)* He fired you?

TYRONE: No. That's not what happened. Ha! You might say *he* got fired, as in really fired! Burnt to the ground fired . . . I'll tell you about it. Don't look nervous, Saul. I'm not gonna say anything bad about Jews. I think he was a *good* guy, at least by the standards of that time. He was kindly, seemed to like me. It was my first job, right out of high school. Took a while before I got the next one! *(Pause.)* I'll tell you one thing. It felt good to walk into that store holding an ad from the classifieds, lookin' for some way to get started in life, and, then, to get hired. It was back in 1967 . . .

TYRONE and SAUL exit.

The End

Postscript to "Manny Wolf - Tyrone Young"

The opening scene of "Manny Wolf – Tyrone Young" relates the sad, scary situation faced by the predominantly white business owners in downtown Newark in the years leading up to the Black protest riots during the summer of 1967. The first scene departs from actual fact only slightly: It was Al, not Manny, who was kicked out of an office of the Metropolitan Life Insurance Company when he mentioned the High Holy Days. Also, unlike Manny, Al didn't graduate from Fordham. He attended night classes at NYU but never received a degree. The most striking circumstance in the first scene is absolutely true: The Manny Wolf character felt the need to put money in the pouch of his collector to reduce the chance that the collector would be harmed when he was waylaid by hoodlums. The scene that takes place on the day of the riot and all subsequent events are fictional.

The play is ethically complex and, I think, painful for Jews. Manny Wolf is a decent human being with a high level of moral awareness. However, he regularly cheats many of his customers. His excuse—the extra difficulty running a business in the Central District—carries some weight. But what he does is still unethical.

Rosie, Manny's Black store manager, is also implicated in the immoral practices, as was my father. Al willingly sold to many store owners who routinely overcharged their Black customers. In conversations with the family, Al did not hide the fact that he was bothered by this.

Manny is right in that it was definitely time for white store owners to leave the Black neighborhoods of Newark. The tragedy is that Rosie doesn't get to take over the business. The conclusion of the play is hopeful. With the passing of years, Tyrone has become a successful Newark entrepreneur.

There is much to Manny's comment that he was "left with the dirty end of capitalism." The unethical business practices of corporate America, which were enormous back then and not so small now, were carried out in handsome offices high above street level.

I enjoyed writing the play's conclusion in which Saul, the Jewish real estate attorney, is deferential to Tyrone, who is obviously an important client.

Because I've sequenced these plays in rough chronological order, we've reached the end of the time period in which my father appears as a main character. But I'll complete the picture of my father with a story that is closely related, although not part of, "Manny Wolf – Tyrone Young." I was living at home during the summer of 1967, about to return to the University of Rochester for my senior year. On the Saturday after the day in which the Newark riot began, Sally, my brother Mitchell, and I joined Al in his car for a family outing—I think we were driving into New York City for theater. We immediately saw a bullet hole just above and to the left of where my father was sitting in the driver's seat. Around the hole radiated splintered and fractured glass, although the windshield itself was intact. Sally cried out, "What's that!?"

Al responded, "I was on Springfield Avenue when the trouble started. I was stopped at a traffic light. And 'bing!'" That was about all he had to say. I cannot tell you why, but Al had not previously mentioned the bullet, although there would certainly have been much dinner-table discussion about the riot itself. When we asked questions about the bullet, he elaborated slightly. "I think it came from a window on the upper floor of one of the buildings." It had been 20 plus years, but Al knew a thing or two about sniper fire. I won't tell more stories, but Al seemed to disregard personal safety. He continued doing business on the rough streets of Newark, Paterson, and other cities for the rest of his career.

Jewish Florida

Florida is an important component of American Jewish culture, and it shows up in later plays as well as here. Therefore, I'll talk a little bit about it. Jewish Florida consists geographically of South Florida along the east coast. The mostly elderly Jews live in retirement communities or retirement-friendly communities differentiated by economic bracket from modest (Century Village) to luxurious (Boca Raton). My parents provide a perfectly good example. Sally and Al moved to Buttonwood, a development of handsome, not-too-large, vaguely Spanish-style homes in the city of Greenacres in Palm Beach County. To live there, you needed to be 55 or older. Social life revolved around the clubhouse. Some folks rode around in adult tricycles. There was a little lake with a fountain.

Similar developments were being built everywhere, erasing the natural environment or co-existing somewhat uncomfortably with the remnants of it. There were small- to medium-size alligators in the lake, and lots of rattlesnakes if you ventured beyond the paved roads. During my visits, I encountered them regularly while jogging. Sometimes, just for fun, I'd find a long stick and provoke the snake into striking the stick.

The "snowbirds" maintained their homes up North and just wintered in Florida. But sooner or later, the snowbirds moved to Florida full time. Many Jews from Rolling Hills moved to Jewish Florida, so when I visited my parents, I was just a few miles away from some of the folks who were on my paper route when I was a boy. In addition, two of my mother's three sisters, including my aunt Florence (with her husband, my Uncle Joe) moved close by.

Along with the retirees, there were men and women raising families and going off to work in Jewish Florida, but the old Jews did not notice them. These regular-age people, in turn, found the old Jews very annoying. They were terrible drivers. Most, like my mother, were timid and drove much too slowly. Some, like Uncle Joe, drove recklessly and paid little or no attention when they crossed intersections. The old Jews carelessly blocked the aisles of supermarkets with their shopping carts. At the cineplex, they'd forget what movie they'd come to see. They'd shout through the glass window to the young woman or man selling tickets, "We want to see that movie . . . You know which one . . . the one with the big star." Tough on the ticket seller and the other folks standing in the line. Many Latinx people did service work for these old Jews. They were gardeners, maintenance workers, etc. Whatever their opinions, they kept them to themselves.

Wasserman the Water Chemist

A 10-minute play by

David K. Farkas

Setting:

Campus buildings of a university in a mid-size city in New York State.

Characters:

Seth Wasserman: A college student.

Roger, Aaron, and **Katie:** Also college students and friends of Seth.

Dr. Lewis: Faculty member in the chemistry department (any gender).

Narrator: Can be played by "Dr. Lewis."

✱✱✱

[Scene 1]

The NARRATOR enters.

NARRATOR: It is the year 1966 on the campus of Masconig University, located in the city of Masconig, in Central New York State. Roger, Aaron, Katie, and Seth are second-year students who have returned to campus for spring semester after the winter break.

The NARRATOR exits. AARON, ROGER, and KATIE enter.

AARON: Seth dropped out of pre-med. He must have flunked the final in Chordate Anatomy.

ROGER: I thought he was doing OK in Chordate.

KATIE: Me too. His GPA is high.

ROGER: He didn't have any trouble with Organic Chemistry.

AARON: Well, I heard he dropped pre-med.

  SETH enters.

ROGER: Hey, Wasserman. Did you drop out of pre-med?

SETH: Yes.

ROGER: Why?!

SETH: I don't want to be a doctor.

AARON: What? You're a Jewish guy from New York City, and you don't want to be a doctor? New York Jews *wash* out of pre-med. They don't *drop out* if they are doing well in their classes.

ROGER: Your parents having financial problems? There are always loans—even for med school.

SETH: Nothing like that. I decided I don't want to be a doctor.

AARON: You gonna be a pharmaceutical salesman?

ROGER: A folksinger?

KATIE: Why are you guys making so much trouble for Seth? . . . *(In a studied tone of voice.)* Seth, I'd be interested in hearing why you're no longer interested in a medical career and what your current plans might be.

SETH: I'm going to study ecology. I'm going to help protect the environment.

AARON: What's ecology?

ROGER: Dumbass, it's the study of "eeks." Eek-ology. But Seth, what are eeks? Do we have any eeks in New York State?

KATIE: Roger, you're the dumbass.

SETH: Ecology means how natural and man-made systems interact, how they fit together. In particular, I'm looking at how industrialization is harming the environment.

AARON: What environment?

SETH: Like what's all around us—the air, the water. Water pollution is becoming a terrible problem. Air pollution, too.

ROGER: Doesn't that stuff just take care of itself?

KATIE: Seth, do you mean something like "conservation"?

SETH: Kinda. But "conservation" is an old-fashioned term. It doesn't get at how one problem is tied to another problem. Ecology is a systems approach.

KATIE: Do they even teach that here?

SETH: No, not really. Officially, I'll be a chemistry major. I'll be working a lot with Dr. Lewis and Dr. Hamid—they're the department's water chemists. Dr. Lewis is especially interested in ecology. I got interested in it when my T.A. in Organic Chemistry told me about her work. So, I dropped in at her office hours, and we started talking. I'll do some independent studies courses with them. I'll take biology courses. There are two systems engineering courses in the Industrial Engineering department. I'll need statistics. Maybe a course or two in political science. I'll be ready to work as an ecologist.

AARON: Is this any kind of paid work?

SETH: I hope so. Maybe big companies will want to hire ecologists to help them understand how their operations affect the environment. Maybe government. I don't exactly know.

ROGER: Well, maybe ecology can be your side gig. You'll support your family as a folksinger.

AARON: Have you told your parents yet?

SETH: Yep. That's what winter break was all about in the Wasserman household. Arguing with me, pleading with me—every day I was home. It was tag-team: First my dad. Then my mom. Then my dad again. When they weren't arguing with me, they walked around the house like someone had just died.

AARON: I sure wouldn't want to take that bit of news home. "Mom, Dad, I hate to shatter all your hopes and dreams—but, I'm not going to be a doctor like you were planning on since I was a child."

AARON pretends to be SETH'S father. Full of grief, he addresses KATIE, as though she were his wife.

AARON: He doesn't want to be a doctor! And he's always been a smart boy. What did we do wrong?

SETH: That's about the picture.

ROGER: Man, it's tough for Jews, for the guys anyway. Whatever major *I* decide on, my parents won't think too much about it.

KATIE: So, at least do Jewish *women* get a pass on this craziness?

AARON: No way! For the women, it's *marry* a doctor.

ROGER: You know, "the times they are a-changing." Maybe in a few years all those Jewish women will be looking to marry an ecologist. Seth, you'll have more girls than you can handle.

SETH: I don't think I should count on that.

KATIE: Well, whatever the Jewish women decide about marrying ecologists, I think it's great that Seth has his own idea for what he wants to do and that he's going after it.

[Scene 2]

SETH and KATIE, with their textbooks and wire-bound notebooks, are seated together behind a long table in the student union. Two other chairs are vacant. SETH is reading. KATIE is reading and taking notes. Subtly her affection for SETH is revealed. SETH has a cup of coffee. He also has two quart-size jars full of dirty water with sediment and debris visible at the bottom. AARON and ROGER enter.

AARON: Hi, Seth . . . Hey, Katie.

KATIE: Hi.

ROGER: You guys up for a study break? If not we'll move right along.

SETH: A study break sounds good. Grab a seat.

AARON and ROGER sit. They can't help but notice the two jars.

ROGER: What's that?

SETH: Water samples from the Masconig. I filled one jar upstream of the International Polymer plant and the other about 100 yards downstream of IP. There are pollutants in the first sample, but there's much worse stuff in the downstream sample. So all those pipes going into the river from the plant are polluting the river. Also, I've talked to a few guys who work there. I'm learning about how much bad stuff they pump into the river.

ROGER: What's the big deal? No one fishes in that river. Doesn't it all wash out to the ocean anyway?

SETH: Maybe people *could* fish in the Masconig. The Indians sure did. Maybe people could swim in the river some day. Anyway the chemicals flow from the Masconig all the way down the Hudson and into the ocean. And it's not just the water. Animals eat the fish. Pollutants get into the soil.

AARON: Well, that man's an ecologist. What do you think about all this, Katie?

KATIE: Maybe fighting for the environment is like political activism. If wars kill people, so does pollution—just slower, and you can't see it. If we protest to achieve social justice, we can fight for a better environment.

ROGER: *(Ironically.)* Oh. Yeah! You go to the SDS guys with that. They'll love it. Forget Vietnam. Forget Civil Rights. What we really need to protest is dirty water.

SETH: The connection between the environment and social justice isn't that far-fetched. Political activists might listen to environmentalists some day.

[Scene 3]

SETH sits across from DR. LEWIS in her faculty office.

DR. LEWIS: I'm sorry, Seth. Really sorry. But your independent studies plan was not approved.

SETH: What?

81

DR. LEWIS: I heard from Dr. Johnson. It's definite. International Polymer found out about your research, and someone from IP talked to Johnson. This department would barely exist if we didn't get money—all kinds of money—from IP. From other companies too, but a whole lot from IP.

SETH: What should I do?

DR. LEWIS: I don't know.

SETH thinks hard and gathers his resolution.

SETH: I do. I'm going to finish the project. Credit or no credit. No one is going to stop me from working in the lab—are they?

DR. LEWIS: You're not supposed to be doing unauthorized work in the lab. But I'm way too busy to notice who's doing what. Keep a low profile. If you need help with the stats, we can talk.

SETH: Thanks, Dr. Lewis. I want my research to make a difference. I'm going to make that happen.

DR. LEWIS: Seth, I don't think you see the difficulties here. In a rudimentary way, your data make a strong case. But no journal will publish this. The reviewers will say, "You've shown that a study *should* be done." A publishable study would require much more extensive data collection, river flow measurements, a more complete chemical analysis— things no undergraduate can do. And no one in this department—not Dr. Hamid, not me, not anyone—is going to buck the chair and help you turn your bottles of water into a research publication. I'm sorry, Seth. That's just how it is.

SETH: If the research is basically sound, I can go to the newspapers with it.

DR. LEWIS: Maybe, but International Polymer is all over this town. Newspaper **exposé**? I don't think it's gonna happen . . . Seth, the environmental movement is just beginning. Someday we'll be able to take on big corporations. Someday people will listen to us. But that's going to be years from now. If this is what you want to do with your life, you need to be ready for opposition, for disappointments. Do you understand? Are you ready for all that?

SETH: Dr. Lewis, I can handle anything.

DR. LEWIS: *(Laughing slightly.)* Huh! You can? How do you know that?

SETH: When I switched my career plan from pre-med to ecology, I fought with my parents for two weeks during winter break. They love me, but it was the biggest blow-up we ever had. Then, there were family friends—people who've known me all my life . . .

> SETH stands, stretches his body, and then looks down at an imaginary SETH in his chair. He pokes emphatically with his forefinger.

SETH: "Seth, once you give up pre-med, you'll never get another chance at medicine. In a few years this environmental thing may be forgotten, then what? Don't ruin your life, boy" . . . Then it was my relatives when the family got together over the holidays. Even my Uncle Irving, who sorts mail for the Post Office, knows better than me what I should study in college . . . After hearing from my mom that I don't want to be a doctor, my aunts didn't want to look straight at me. It wasn't pretty, Dr. Lewis. But here I am. You might say I'm already a battle-hardened ecologist.

DR. LEWIS: As bad as that! At war with your whole family? Wow!

SETH: Yes. Except for my grandmother.

DR. LEWIS: Your grandmother. What did she say?

SETH: With everyone giving me grief, she took me aside. She said, "'Wasserman.' In Yiddish that means 'water man.' Maybe there's some significance to that. Maybe this is what you were meant to do."

DR LEWIS: What did you say to her?

SETH: Nothing. I just kissed her. She's right, of course. I know my future—Wasserman, the Water Man.

The End

Postscript to "Wasserman the Water Chemist"

"Wasserman the Water Chemist" was written for and performed at the campaign kick-off for an environmental activist and university faculty member, Tracy Furutani, who was running for a position on the Lake Forest Park, Washington, city council. I was asked to write an environmentally themed play for this event. I'd never before written on a topic that had been chosen for me, and I puzzled over an idea for the play. A complicating factor was that most of the folks who would be in the audience knew more about environmental issues and environmental science than I do. What did I have to say to them?

Being one of the oldest members of this group, I decided to write about something they had not experienced: the earliest days of the modern environmental movement. So the play is set in 1966, four years before the first Earth Day made the general public aware of environmental concerns. I told how, as a second-year student at the University of Rochester, my friends and I first heard the words "environment" and "ecology" used as we regularly use them today.

Seth is based on a real person. We later heard that he earned one of the first Ph.D.'s in environmental science. Roughly speaking, I am Aaron. Some of the dialogue in Scenes 1 and 2 is nearly verbatim. My friends and I thought that Seth's jars of dirty water from the Genesee River were among the silliest things we'd ever seen. Fifty years later, as a member of Lake Forest Park Streamkeepers, I tested the water quality of our local streams. The joke's on me.

The script, when I finished it, was problematic. It was a Jewish play as much (or more) than it was an environmental play. After some hesitation, the decision was made to perform it. Quite remarkably, a Jewish pre-med student and his non-Jewish fiancé played Seth and Katie. Tracy played Dr. Lewis and was addressed as "Dr. Furutani" in our performance. I played "Aaron." It all went over well—plus Tracy was elected!

Jews and medicine

A Jewish joke:

A woman is attending the inauguration of her son as President of the United States. He will be the first Jewish president. Someone congratulates her, "You must be so proud of your son!" She replies, "Yes, yes. But his brother. He's a doctor!"

Even as a boy, I understood the deep-rooted connection between Jews and medicine. It was explained to me that Jews were often expelled from the countries they lived in. If you owned land, if you had a business, it was all lost to you. If you were a doctor, you could leave and set up your practice elsewhere—much as Malachi does in "Malachi in the Time of Plague." A medical degree even puts you on an even footing with the "Walters" of the world. Walters, like everyone else, become ill, and a good doctor is respected and valued, even with a Semitic nose or a heavy Jewish accent.

As reflected in "Wasserman the Water Chemist," my parents were bitterly disappointed when I announced that I was giving up pre-med (to major in English—and ultimately to continue on to a doctorate). Seth's speeches about the grief he got from his family were my experiences (minus the supportive grandmother). My mother, just months before her death at the age of 95, would still not give it up, "OK, you became a doctor. But not a *doctor* doctor!"

La Paloma

A 10-minute play by

David K. Farkas

Prequel to "She's a Runner"

Setting:

The language lab in Clifton (New Jersey) High School in the year 1963.

Characters:

David, Vivian, Bud, and **Rhonda**: High school seniors.

The Language Lab: A voice-over, possibly pre-recorded. The Language Lab speaks Castilian Spanish and speaks Castilian-accented English, always slowly and formally. This actor also plays Conformity.

Conformity: The cosmic agent of conformity and the suppression of individual freedom of action and thought. Conformity is a native speaker of mainstream North American English with a refined voice and manner.

Freedom (played by "Vivian"): The cosmic agent of freedom, the true freedom that lives inside us.

Suggested minimum casting:

David
Vivian/Freedom
Rhonda
Bud
The Language Lab/Conformity

VIVIAN and DAVID, a high-school couple, are talking just inside the school's spacious language lab. He is carrying her books as well as his own. Behind them, parallel to the stage backdrop, is a long table with two shoe-box size consoles, each with a coiled electrical cord connected to a headset. Two student chairs, pulled up to the table, face upstage. There is a similar setup that is perpendicular to the backdrop and is positioned either stage left or stage right. (The chairs face offstage). The audience may be asked to stand and join hands to make a ring around the stage.

VIVIAN: I don't see what you're always complaining about. Why are you so . . . *bored* with everything? The new high school is super-cool—everyone likes it. It's a "campus." If we want to, we can go out one of the doors and walk from Wing A to Wing B during class change. You sure couldn't do that in the old building . . . The marching band is going to the Rose Bowl—that's a big honor.

DAVID: Same old stupid teachers. I actually don't care about the marching band or even the high school. There's more going on than just high school. Do you know who Allen Ginsberg is?

VIVIAN: Yes, I know who Allen Ginsberg is.

DAVID: Have you read any of his poems?

VIVIAN: No, I haven't read any of his stupid poems. You don't like me any more because I haven't read Allen Ginsberg's poems?

DAVID: I didn't say that.

VIVIAN: And a good thing too! *(Pause.)* Even looking beyond high school, I mean at *everything*, the whole country, things seem pretty good. John F. Kennedy is president. Eisenhower was old and boring. But Kennedy isn't boring. He started the Peace Corps.

DAVID: OK. That's at least something.

RHONDA and BUD approach, each carrying some books.

RHONDA: Ready for an hour of language lab?

VIVIAN: I guess. I'm not sure how much Spanish we're learning, but it's pretty neat not having any teacher. I mean, just talking to the computer. That's like . . . amazing.

DAVID and VIVIAN take seats at the upstage table (their backs face the audience). RHONDA and BUD take their seats and face stage left or stage right. All four put on their headsets, with DAVID exhibiting reluctance. As they speak, they look straight ahead and seem to be talking to their console.

LANGUAGE LAB (V.O.): Bienvenido al laboratorio de idiomas. Hoy aprendemos la palabra "paloma." Repite . . . La paloma.

ALL: La paloma.

LANGUAGE LAB (V.O.): La paloma. The dove. Repite.

ALL: La paloma. The dove.

LANGUAGE LAB (V.O.): De nuevo. La paloma. The dove. Repite.

DAVID is becoming visibly impatient.

ALL: La paloma. The dove.

LANGUAGE LAB (V.O.): Bueno. Repite. La paloma.

ALL: La paloma.

LANGUAGE LAB (V.O.): Muy bueno! Repite. La paloma.

VIVIAN, BUD, RHONDA: La paloma.	**DAVID:** La paloma. La paloma. La paloma.

LANGUAGE LAB (V.O.): Otra vez. La paloma. The dove. Repite.

DAVID is growing very agitated.

VIVIAN, BUD, RHONDA: La paloma. The dove.	**DAVID:** *(Louder.)* La paloma. La paloma . . . La Maloma! La Baloma!!

LANGUAGE LAB (V.O.): Otra vez. La paloma. The dove. Repite.

DAVID throws down his headset and stands. Somehow he still hears the LANGUAGE LAB.

LANGUAGE LAB (V.O.): Otra vez. La paloma. The dove. Repite.

VIVIAN, BUD, RHONDA: La paloma. The dove.

DAVID: *(Screaming.)* La paloma. La Baloma. La Pashmola! La Shmagola!

LANGUAGE LAB (V.O.): Muy bueno! Repite. La paloma. The dove.

> DAVID goes completely berserk. He shouts "La Paloma," The dove," "Otra vez," and anything else the actor chooses. VIVIAN has become aware that DAVID has gone berserk. She slowly removes her headset and turns toward him. BUD and RHONDA don't notice anything and continue with the exercise.

BUD, RHONDA: La paloma. The dove.

LANGUAGE LAB (V.O.): Otra vez. La paloma. The dove. Repite.

BUD, RHONDA: La paloma. The dove.

> VIVIAN approaches DAVID. Trying to calm him, she places her hands on his shoulders.

LANGUAGE LAB (V.O.): Muy bueno! Repite. La paloma. The dove.

BUD, RHONDA: La paloma. Repite. The dove. Repite.

> In a crazed manner, DAVID starts flapping his arms like wings, still screaming but now with the addition of frantic bird sounds. VIVIAN now joins him. They run all over the language lab like crazed doves. BUD and RHONDA don't notice anything.

LANGUAGE LAB (V.O.): Otra vez. La paloma.

BUD, RHONDA: La paloma.

> DAVID and VIVIAN approach RHONDA and draw her attention from the console. They look hard into her face. She responds, loses control, and joins them. The three crazed doves run around the room screaming and making bird sounds.

LANGUAGE LAB (V.O.): The dove. Repite.

BUD: The dove.

LANGUAGE LAB (V.O.): Muy bueno! Muy bueno! Repite. The dove. The dove. La paloma.

DAVID, VIVIAN, and RHONDA now approach BUD and draw his attention from the exercise. RHONDA, in particular, looks hard into his face, flapping her wings wildly.

LANGUAGE LAB (V.0.): Otra vez. La paloma. The dove.

BUD responds, starts flapping his arms like wings, stands, and joins them.

LANGUAGE LAB (V.0.): De nuevo. La paloma. The dove. La paloma. La paloma. The dove. The dove. La paloma. The dove. Repite.

The four students are flying around the room in complete hysteria. They are looking for a way to escape the language lab.

STUDENTS AS DOVES: *(In a hysterical jumble of words and actions.)* La paloma. The dove. Repite. La paloma. Let me out of here! La paloma. The dove. Freedom! Give me freedom. The dove. La paloma. Otra vez. Is this a window? La Paloma. The dove. Repite.

LANGUAGE LAB (V.0.): Otra vez. La paloma.

The four crazed doves fly around the language lab in a loose formation, then individually seem to find various ways to escape the language lab. They joyfully exit the stage in various directions. One or two may escape down the aisles into the audience.

LANGUAGE LAB (V.0.): Otra vez. La paloma. The dove. Repite. Muy Bueno. Muy Bueno.

CONFORMITY enters. He/she/they is sardonic and malevolent. CONFORMITY addresses the audience. If there has been applause because audience members thought the play had ended, CONFORMITY begins with "Stop!" to still the applause.

CONFORMITY: [Stop!] This story is *not over.* What? You think the world is so generous, so accommodating? You think that the four doves will take wing and find their freedom? You think that the four students will get away with not following the rules? No, it doesn't work that way. Please allow me to introduce myself. I appear in infinite forms. But in each of them my mission is to destroy the human spirit. At the present moment, you can call me "Conformity." My task right now is a small one—enforcing the rules of the language lab and the high school. Next month, when John F. Kennedy is assassinated, I will have a different name and a larger task. I will direct the rifle shots of Lee Harvey Oswald.

> The four doves return to the stage, flapping their wings calmly. Initially, they are simply obedient, but as they approach CONFORMITY, they become tense, then frightened. CONFORMITY picks up a rifle by means of a stage trick. Making frantic bird sounds, the doves now try desperately to evade CONFORMITY, but they are trapped inside the language lab searching for a door, a window, or some other way to escape. Wielding the rifle, CONFORMITY calmly and confidently pursues the trapped doves. CONFORMITY corners RHONDA-DOVE and shoots her at close range. With a tragic motion, she falls lifeless to the ground. Conformity speaks his Spanish words without a trace of a Spanish accent.

CONFORMITY: Bueno!

> The remaining three doves are still more terrified, as is reflected in their increasingly frantic efforts to evade CONFORMITY. CONFORMITY corners and shoots BUD-DOVE. RHONDA-DOVE and BUD-DOVE sit up to watch what ensues, providing a hint that the denouement will not be so grim.

CONFORMITY: Otra vez.

> Cornered by CONFORMITY, DAVID-DOVE and VIVIAN-DOVE clasp each other in a close embrace, whimpering in fear. CONFORMITY sends a single bullet through both of them. They drop to the ground quickly and silently. Conformity looks down at his victims.

CONFORMITY: *(With sardonic laughter.)* Bueno . . . Bueno.

> CONFORMITY turns to the audience with a long, baleful glance. DAVID-DOVE and VIVIAN-DOVE sit up.

CONFORMITY: *(Turning now to address all four.)* Bud, Rhonda, Vivian, David—I am the cosmic principle of Conformity. I restrict and brutally punish all independent thinking and free expression—in the schools, in corporations, in government, especially when a nation's leaders decide to go to war. Do you understand what this means?

[In place of "sir," the response can be "ma'am" or something else.]

ALL: Yes, sir.

CONFORMITY: I reign supreme in Clifton High School. Is this fully acknowledged?

ALL: Yes, sir.

CONFORMITY: You are young. Do you want your lives restored? I am willing to do this.

ALL: *(Fervently.)* Yes, sir.

CONFORMITY: You do understand that you are students at Clifton High School, where wayward, individualistic behavior is not tolerated?

ALL: *(Fervently.)* Yes, sir.

CONFORMITY: Bud, you will conform in all things? You will never question a rule. Never question what a teacher says.

BUD: *(Fervently.)* Yes, sir.

CONFORMITY: Rhonda, you will conform in all things?

RHONDA: *(Fervently.)* Yes, sir.

CONFORMITY: Vivian, you will conform in all things?

VIVIAN: *(Fervently.)* Yes, sir.

CONFORMITY: David. You, the ringleader—the one who initially expressed dissatisfaction with the language lab. Have you changed your attitude?

DAVID: *(Fervently.)* Yes, sir.

CONFORMITY: David. Tell me your feelings about the Clifton High School Fighting Mustang Marching Band.

DAVID: *(Fervently.)* One hundred and twenty students marching in unison—what could be better than that! . . . Sir.

CONFORMITY: All right then. You may return to your stations in the language lab. The word of the day will be "La paloma." The dove.

> The students willingly return to their stations, put on their headsets, and listen attentively for the word they know will come.

CONFORMITY: La paloma. The dove.

ALL: La paloma. The dove.

CONFORMITY: Otra vez. La paloma. The dove.

ALL: La paloma. The dove.

CONFORMITY: La paloma. The dove. Repite.

> Unnoticed by CONFORMITY, VIVIAN sets down her headset, leaves her station, and stands upstage of CONFORMITY. With a slow dramatic gesture, she rises to her full height and spreads her arms wide. Everyone freezes. Then she speaks.

VIVIAN AS FREEDOM: David!

> DAVID hears her, sets down his headset, and rises to approach her, filled with awe. CONFORMITY, VIVIAN, and BUD remain frozen and oblivious.

DAVID: Yes.

VIVIAN AS FREEDOM: I am Freedom, the true freedom that lives inside us. I don't snarl, I whisper. I offer a promise of better days. Remember me, David.

> DAVID nods solemnly and emphatically in response. VIVIAN and DAVID return to their stations, but they sit silently looking at each other and do not put on their headsets.

CONFORMITY: La paloma. The dove.

BUD, RHONDA: La paloma. The dove.

CONFORMITY: *(Not noticing VIVIAN and DAVID.)* Bueno.

DAVID: *(To himself and to the audience.)* It can't happen now. It can't happen here. But one day I will be free.

Once more, VIVIAN stands, rises to her full height, and spreads her arms wide.

VIVIAN AS FREEDOM: Yes, David!

The End

Postscript to "La Paloma"

I began my senior year in Clifton (NJ) High School in a new, very modern building. Even I, who hated almost everything about high school, was impressed. The pride of the new high school, the Big Thing, was the computer. As you entered the high school through the front doors, several refrigerator-size tape drives with rows of blinking lights were in full view behind a glass wall. We would now receive computer-printed report cards rather than report cards with grades filled out in ink by our teachers. The computer also did something else that—until we learned better—was very exciting: It powered the much-anticipated language lab.

But nothing really improved. We had the same benighted teachers and the same ossified rules. I'll allow myself just one story: I joined the History Club. The club consisted entirely of college-bound students who had been told that colleges wanted evidence that you were "well rounded." I had somehow been elected treasurer during the first meeting, and so just before the second meeting the teacher handed me a slip of paper consisting of the treasurer's report: "The History Club has twenty-four dollars and sixty-seven cents in the treasury." She emphasized that I was to deliver the treasurer's report verbatim—absolutely no deviations from the written text. I tried, but lost the struggle. I changed the sentence to something like "There's twenty-four dollars and sixty-seven cents in the treasury of the History Club."—and earned a week in detention. I didn't much mind the punishment. The detention hall, with its assortment of serious ruffians, was one of the few interesting places in the school. Plus, the detention monitor was a teacher I liked, Mr. Zuluski, who ran the debate club. Mr. Zuluski was a kindly and thoughtful man who served as detention monitor because he'd been a boxer before turning to teaching.

"La Paloma" is not a Jewish play, but it is included in this collection because it's a kind of prequel to "She's a Runner, the play that appears next. The David of "She's a Runner" is independent-minded and rebellious in spirit, but he exhibits these qualities in a mature and judicious manner. He is a successful person who has moved past the desperation and anger that characterizes the David of "La Paloma."

She's a Runner

A 10-minute play by

David K. Farkas

Setting:

A senior residence in an upscale suburb north of New York City..

Characters:

David Abrams: Casually dressed, in his thirties.
Betty Goldman: In her 90s and living in the senior residence.
Ms. Richards: The manager of the senior residence.

✲✲✲

DAVID and MS. RICHARDS are standing in the reception area.

MS. RICHARDS: I hope you had a good visit with your grandmother.

DAVID: Yes, I did. She gets confused at moments, but for the most part, she's pretty sharp . . . Actually, she's not my grandmother. She's my great aunt. Rachel, her daughter, is my mother's cousin.

MS. RICHARDS: That's wonderful. A lot of our residents don't get many visits even from their children and grandchildren.

DAVID: Well, I saw her often when I was growing up. I've always felt close to her. I call her "Aunt Betty," just like my mother did.

MS. RICHARDS: Well, thank you for visiting. I hope you come again soon.

DAVID: Yes, I certainly hope to. I grew up in New Jersey, but I live in Seattle, and I'm not on the East Coast that often. Ben and Rachel are in Florida right now. Otherwise, they'd be here with me.

MS. RICHARDS: My husband and I have been to Seattle several times. Do you work in computers?

DAVID: A lot of people *do* work in high tech, but I don't. There's only one jazz club left in the whole city, and that's my club. One question: Why is there a red border around Betty's name tag? I didn't see that with the other residents.

MS. RICHARDS: Oh, just an administrative thing. Certain residents have colored borders on their badge—for different purposes. Like . . . medication schedules.

DAVID: OK. So what does Betty's red border mean?

MS. RICHARDS: Well . . . It means she's a runner.

DAVID: She's what?

MS. RICHARDS: Betty Goldman has a history of leaving the building—the entire property in fact—without authorization. Not easy for a woman with a walker and an oxygen concentrator, but she manages it.

DAVID: I'm not entirely surprised.

MS. RICHARDS: Betty isn't strong enough to open the outer door. It's actually designed that way. And, of course, our staff would never permit her to leave the building. But Betty tries to slip past the reception desk and follow visitors out of the building. Usually it's a delivery person.

DAVID: Do Rachel and Ben know she's a "runner"?

MS. RICHARDS: Of course.

DAVID: Betty said something about being in a police station. I *assumed* this was something she imagined. *Did* she slip through the door and wind up in a police station?

MS. RICHARDS: This is awkward. But . . . yes.

DAVID: Wow, so she really is a runner! How often does she run? How many times has she slipped past you folks?

MS. RICHARDS: Mr. Abrams. Our staff is well-trained and alert. But Betty is very . . . if I may use the word, sneaky. She's actually our most successful runner. She's left the building four times this year, and three of those times she left the premises. I want you to understand: It did not take long for us to notice that she was gone. The staff responded quickly, and we did everything we could to locate her. When we found her, we made sure that the return was gentle and friendly. The border on her name badge is one of the ways we're addressing the problem.

DAVID: But she *did* get as far as the police station. Or, far enough to wind up at the police station. Do Rachel and Ben know about that incident?

MS. RICHARDS: Mr. Abrams. Actually, they don't. We provide them with . . . general . . . information about these incidents. When I explain, they don't ask a lot of questions, and I don't see any need to upset them with details when they were . . . not showing that much interest.

DAVID: *(Chuckling.)* They *might* have shown interest if you'd told them about the police station.

MS. RICHARDS: Mr. Abrams, David. Mr. and Ms. Schwartz are somewhat difficult clients. I think you can guess what I'm referring to. They don't always understand the complexities of managing a facility like this one. They've talked about moving Betty to another senior residence. It might be in everyone's interest if you don't mention any of this to them.

DAVID: I do understand what you mean. I'm in the process of forgetting entirely that Betty has achieved notable success as a runner. But, it won't be *my* fault if Betty mentions the police station to Rachel.

MS. RICHARDS: I'm pretty confident she's not going to do that. Betty knows how to keep her secrets, and she does like living here. She likes *us*. And, despite the extra trouble she's caused, I really like Betty. We talk from time to time.

DAVID: Well, then. I'll tell you something. In a way, Betty has always been a "runner." She's always looked for opportunities to escape what to her were restrictions, walls. When she was a young woman—and she was a beautiful young woman—she worked for a company that sold fine fabrics—to couturiers. The owner, a woman, took a real interest in Betty. Took her to parties in Greenwich Village—the real Bohemian life. Betty never went to college, but she was always well read, and she's always

99

had . . . you might say . . . a natural grace. We don't know how far it went, but she was definitely part of the Village scene—until the family found out. Then it ended.

MS. RICHARDS: I had no idea. But I do understand the "natural grace" you're talking about.

DAVID: Then she married Harry. That was the conventional thing to do, and she did it. Harry was handsome, and had a business, a children's clothing store. He was a good man, but . . . she would have liked more from the marriage.

MS. RICHARDS: Yes, I've heard about Harry.

DAVID: When Rachel met Ben, Harry was dead set against the marriage. Ben was really, really poor. His people were from the Lower East Side, worked in the garment district. No one knew that he'd be successful. He was in the army at the time. Betty helped Rachel elope. Ben had been sent to Germany. Betty had enough of her own money for a plane ticket. Ben and Rachel were married by the Jewish chaplain right on the base. Eloping was really radical back then—in their culture at least. Rachel wouldn't have done it, probably wouldn't have married Ben at all, without Betty.

MS. RICHARDS: I do love Betty!

DAVID: Just one more story. Betty is the only member of the family—well, her and me—who aren't big supporters of Israel. Betty will say she's "sympathetic" with the Palestinians. Just a few years back, when Ben, Rachel, their kids, and Betty all took a big trip to Israel, Betty said she wanted to see the West Bank. You can imagine how that went over. So, one morning, Betty left the hotel, found a Palestinian cab driver, and had him take her to Ramallah—for the whole day. Betty didn't have a cell phone, so she didn't call. The family went nuts not knowing where she was. But Betty got a good look at Ramallah. She and the cab driver had coffee at a café. Betty talked to all kinds of people that day. Rachel and Ben were furious. So, I do understand. Betty *is* a runner. She's always looked for her chances to be free.

MS. RICHARDS: Well, it's important to keep her safe. But I understand Betty, and I'm glad you understand our situation.

BETTY enters with her walker and her oxygen concentrator. (The oxygen concentrator and especially its cannula) may be imaginary.)

BETTY: Oh, Mrs. Richards. I'm so glad you've met David. He's my grand nephew.

MS. RICHARDS: Yes, Betty. We've had a wonderful talk. About you, in fact.

BETTY: About me? Oh my! Nothing too bad, I hope . . . David, I don't want to keep you, but there is just one more thing I need to show you in my room. Would you come up with me?

DAVID: Sure, Aunt Betty.

DAVID starts to follow her.

MS. RICHARDS: Well, it was so nice to meet you, David.

BETTY leads DAVID to an exit, they cross-over and re-enter on the other side of the stage. MS. RICHARDS exits.

BETTY: David, I want you to take me to the train station. I'm going down to New Orleans to meet old friends. People I haven't seen in many years. I know a way to get out of the building—through a door from the kitchen.

DAVID: New Orleans?

BETTY: Yes, I think . . . New Orleans, but maybe . . . I'm not sure now.

DAVID: Aunt Betty, I think all your old friends agreed they'd each find someplace peaceful, someplace beautiful. Then they'd sit for a long time, and remember the good times you all had together.

BETTY: Maybe . . . Yes. I do think that was the plan.

DAVID: I bet Rachel would take you to a really nice park. I'm sure she would.

BETTY: No, not Rachel. We need to go today. And I want to go with you. Rachel and Ben are about family dinners and doctor visits. You're about feeling free. I want to do this with you. I want to ride down the highway at

70 miles an hour with all the windows open. And not just to a park. I want something bigger, more memorable than that.

DAVID: *(Pointing to the oxygen concentrator.)* Do you know how long the battery lasts on that thing?

BETTY: Five hours. And I know it's charged.

DAVID: You're sure about the battery?

BETTY: David, I'm a very old woman, and I don't have much time left. I think I have one more adventure coming to me, and nobody but you is going to make that happen.

DAVID: You understand, this isn't a small thing. I'm not on any list of people who can take you out of the building. This is a real "jail break." I promise this will not go over well with Ms. Richards. And, she probably won't be able to hide this escapade from Rachel and Ben.

BETTY: We'll take Ms. Richards with us . . . No, she's too busy. But, when we get back, I'll explain. It will be alright.

DAVID: I'm not exactly betting on that. But she does like you. What about Rachel and Ben?

BETTY: What are they going to do to an old lady? I'm the mom. I'll still be the mom. Let's have one really special day together. One really special five hours. I promise I'll be OK.

DAVID: Damn. This is totally crazy, Aunt Betty.

BETTY: No, not crazy. It's living.

DAVID: And it definitely won't be New Orleans.

BETTY: OK, not New Orleans. But it will be a day I won't forget. First we need to go down the elevator to the basement level. You can bring your car around.

DAVID: Yes, Aunt Betty. It will be quite a day. We'll drive up High-Tor Mountain. It looks out over the Hudson. If you want, I'll write down all your memories, and maybe we can send your friends a letter.

BETTY: Yes, a letter, just a short one, to everyone. And better if you do the writing. My hands aren't steady. And better if you *keep* the letter because I don't have a single address. But, yes, a letter. To the people I remember and to the people I've forgotten. To the artists and the poets and the boyfriends of long ago . . . One more thing. I want champagne and two glasses, for a toast.

DAVID: First, the answer is "yes." How could we not? Second, a question. Are you supposed to drink alcohol?

BETTY: No. Alcohol is not on my approved diet, and so I take my meals at tables where they don't serve wine. But . . . no one ever tells me not to drink wine at Passover seders, so I can do two little toasts today. First, a toast to my friends from long ago. Then, a toast to us—to our need to be free and to our special day together.

DAVID: Yes!

They exit.

The End

Postscript to "She's a Runner"

David, in "She's a Runner," is the person I'd like to be. Out of all my 100-plus 10-minute plays, he's one of my very favorite characters. Unfortunately, Dan in "Sunday Walk in North Creek Park" is the person I too often am. Moving forward in this book, you'll see who that fellow is.

The David of "She's a Runner" is perceptive and empathetic. He's no pushover when he insists that Ms. Richards reveal the meaning of Betty's nametag. But he is also tactful, knows not to push too hard, and ultimately establishes a warm, respectful relationship with Ms. Richards.

David is also decisive and brave—willing to assume responsibility for engineering Betty's escape from her senior residence, despite the obvious risk of a medical crisis. At the same time he makes careful judgments about what kind of special day will be possible for Betty, and he exercises rhetorical skills to gracefully reconcile Betty to a scaled down version of the reunion she had envisioned.

The Betty in the play is based on an actual person. She lived in an era when the lives of nearly all women were circumscribed and stunted by society's oppressive rules and traditions. But Betty always sought and sometimes found her freedom, and the stories about Betty related in the play are factual. She did indeed, for a time, escape life in the Bronx to hang out with intellectuals in Greenwich Village. Moreover, I learned during a visit that Betty was indeed a "runner." In my happiest imagination, the event that concludes the play would have really taken place.

David and Betty are kindred spirits. In high-tech Seattle, he runs a jazz club. He deeply understands Betty's impulse to escape, and he even derives mischievous pleasure when he hears of her successes as a runner. He will certainly help Mrs. Richards keep all this hidden from Betty's daughter and husband. The champagne toast they envision on High-Tor Mountain will be a jubilant moment for both Betty and David.

What We Preserve

A 10-minute play by

David K. Farkas

Setting:

A small restaurant, a cocktail lounge, and a park bench—all in South Florida.

Characters:

Sam Gentner: An old man, formerly a big-time real estate developer.
Gabe Rothstein: An old man, formerly a big-time real estate developer.
Matt Gattis: A corrupt Florida State Legislator.
Suzie: A server at a small, nondescript restaurant.
Lila: A sex worker who can often be found in the bars near the Florida Statehouse. (Can be played by "Suzie").

[Scene 1]

SAM sits at a table at the restaurant. He is alert, waiting for something. GABE enters, obviously looking for someone. He spots SAM.

GABE: There you are. You're looking old.

SAM: What did you expect? Sit down.

GABE: Why am I here?

SAM: Yah got so much better stuff to do?

GABE: No.

SAM: Then sit down. I'm buying. Breakfast. Eggs. A muffin. Whatever.

GABE sits. They both look quickly at the menu, not taking much interest.

SAM: You still got it in you for one more deal? A big one? You still got juice in Tallahassee?

GABE: The first question is why I'd work with you. No, the first question is why I'm even here. You double-crossed me.

SAM: That's wrong. You couldn't figure out when to stop. I had to pull the plug on the whole thing and take our profit.

GABE: Barely a profit. You got nervous. No balls. I could've pushed a little harder. They'd have come around.

SAM: Gabe, let's not go through that again. I know what you think. You know what I think. You still got it in you for one more deal?

GABE: Maybe I do. A big deal? I'm not interested in buying some strip mall.

SAM: This ain't a strip mall. If you don't like what I got, it won't be because it's too small. It'll be because it's too big.

GABE: That'd be a first . . . So, tell me already.

SAM: For me, it's about Hannah. All her life I try to give her something—make up for not being such a great father. Condo in a real nice building. Fancy car. Credit card full up with bucks. It's always, "Thanks, Dad. But I don't need that." She lives so simply. There's nothing she needs, nothing she wants. Finally. Finally, she asks me for something: "Save Deacon Island."

GABE: What?

SAM: Save it from development. Make it a preserve, a state park. Something like that. She says that's the one thing my money can do for her. She thinks I can just buy the Island and make it a park. She doesn't understand that no one has *that* much money. But, if you work the politics, and I work the finances—the corporations, the big donors, general obligation munis. Maybe we can do it.

GABE: Why do I care about some swampy island? I'm going hiking, you think?

SAM: No, I'm thinking it's the David Rothstein Nature Preserve or the David Rothstein State Park. A *real* memorial. Not a slab of marble in a cemetery, but a place where people go to enjoy themselves. Your boy would like that.

GABE: I don't know *what* he cared about. Not much actually.

SAM: Well, he was your son, and a real memorial—something to keep his name alive—that has to be a good thing.

GABE shrugs, but his shrug conveys agreement. SUZIE comes to the table.

SUZIE: Hi Sam. Sorry, we're slow today. *(To both men.)* You know what you want?

SAM: Just coffee and a muffin—blueberry if you got it. One check. Gabe?

GABE: Yeah, muffin sounds OK. I take milk with my coffee. Can you warm the muffin?

SUZIE: OK. Won't take too long.

Because SUZIE does not actually appear again in this scene, the actor has time to change her costume to become LILA.

SAM: So, one more deal. For David . . . And Hannah. Let's end on a big one. There's a lot of public support for environmental causes, preserving nature. We just might be able to do it. If not the whole island, part of it. But . . . I'd really like to do the whole damn thing.

GABE: "David N. Rothstein Nature Preserve." There is something to that. I mean, Miriam would like that. Hell, *I'd* like that. But the name, it's *just* named for David?

SAM: Hannah couldn't care less about having her name or the Gentner name on this thing. She probably wouldn't want it. I guess we could put her name on the visitors center. No, not even that. Maybe some stream that runs through the place. Some pond she particularly likes.

GABE: OK. Maybe . . . Yes. One final deal. I'm tired of golf anyway. Tired of the boring conversations in the clubhouse. The gears are starting to turn. I still know how to do this. If it's going well, the guv'nor will sign on—and then take all the credit. But that's OK, as long as we got the name wired in. That's non-negotiable.

SAM: That's right. "David N. Rothstein Nature Preserve." However, you want it, Gabe.

GABE: There are some real SOBs in the Legislature these days. Not just your usual gonifs. They got guys like Matt Gattis now. I'm gonna have to dig deep. Then maybe play a little rough.

SAM: Well, you know how to play the rough game. And it's all for the right reasons. Nature, the environment. Give people a new place to go hiking. I can sell it to corporations, foundations, family trusts. I can definitely sell this.

GABE nods to signal he's signing on.

SAM: Here's Suzie with the muffins.

[Scene 2]

MATT is seated at a table in a cocktail lounge. LILA enters and sits down next to MATT.

MATT: Go away. I'm not interested. Go peddle your goods somewhere else.

LILA: That's not why I'm here. I got a message for you.

MATT: Message? What kind of a message?

LILA: A message that someone will pay me $500 to give to you. Personal delivery, just a few words in your ear.

MATT: Who's the someone?

LILA: Nobody. Just some homeless guy. Someone paid *him* to get *me* to give *you* the message.

MATT: OK. I'm impressed. What's the message?

LILA: The message is: Support the Deacon Island project. Support it strong. Or else all the payoff money you took on the McHenry Bridge. It all comes out. That's it. Support Deacon Island or "McHenry Bridge." There, I've earned my money.

MATT: Fuck! Fuck! Fuck! When hell freezes over. My people hate that damn bill. I'm not gonna do it! What do you know about who's behind this message? You must know something. I got to talk to them. Talk some sense into them.

LILA: I don't know one more thing, dumb-ass. Someone went to a lot of trouble to hide their tracks. Looks to me that someone really wants to put the squeeze on you. I bet that bridge can put you right in jail. Love to see it, Baby!

MATT: Screw you, Lila. Now get outta my face.

LILA: You bet. There's no better way to make 500 bucks than this. I'd have done it for free.

LILA exits.

[Scene 3]

MATT sits somewhere (not in the cocktail lounge). He's talking on a cell phone and is very angry and upset.

MATT: Hannah Gentner dead? How could you be so stupid?

MATT listens.

MATT: That's no reason. You're supposed to know how to do this kinda stuff. I'm trying to get Sam Gentner off my ass with this nature preserve thing, and now this? I'm fucked.

MATT listens.

MATT: Well, that much is good. What I paid you, I guess you're gonna keep. But you're not getting one more dollar. And listen. There's 8 billion people in the world. The last one of those 8 billion people you are ever going to talk to again is me. You got that? Asshole! Fuckin' asshole! Yes, yes, I'm ditching the phone. It's not even mine.

[Scene 4]

SAM and GABE sit on a bench somewhere. They are overwhelmed with grief.

GABE: It wasn't supposed to happen that way. You *know* that. I never thought Gattis would look in your direction. You're a money guy, not a politics guy. Why would he think that *you* were blackmailing him?

SAM: Do we know it was him?

GABE: Not officially. But it has to be connected with Gattis. It looks like a clean hit. Police have nothing to go on. Actually, looks like it wasn't meant to be a hit at all. Probably Gattis just wanted her roughed up. In order to scare you. But she must have had more fight in her than the guy expected, and it all went south.

SAM: She'd fight. She damn well gave him hell.

GABE: I did this, Sam. I never, ever wanted anything like this. To bring Hannah back, I'd put myself in the grave, in a moment—you know that. And I'll roast Matt Gattis. Right now, he's crying the biggest tears for Hannah in the whole Legislature. He'll vote "yes" on the preserve. With Hannah's photo being shown on TV, a bunch of them will vote yes. I'll wait for his vote. But unless he wants to live in North Korea, he's headed for jail for the bridge payoffs. You have my guarantee on that.

SAM: I got nothing now. I had a daughter. I didn't always understand her, but—oh—how I loved her. And Louise—I got no wife either. She's just walking dead, walking straight to the cemetery. I got nothing.

GABE: I know. I know how it feels. But Hannah lived 40 years. That's a lifetime she lived. And she was happy. And it was a lifetime for you to be a father. I lost David when he was 20. And things never were right with him, except when he was a young boy.

SAM: This was the one thing she ever wanted from me. The one thing I could ever give her—try to give her. And we killed her. Gabe, we killed her.

GABE: You know, we've got the preserve. We've *got* it. The "Hannah Gentner-David Rothstein Nature Preserve." No one is fighting against it now. They'll be stuff about both of them in the visitors center. And you know what else? Saving Deacon Island is what mattered to her—maybe more than her life. Somewhere—maybe looking down from heaven—she's saying, "Dad, this was an OK deal for me."

SAM: Gabe, I don't want to hear about your damn "heaven." I don't believe in any heaven. I believe in the actual world we all live in, and I got nothing. That's what I got. In the real world Hannah never even knew she'd get that park. She knew I was fighting for it. That *we* were fighting for it. But she didn't know we'd win.

GABE: Yes, she did. OK, you don't got to listen to me about heaven. But Hannah had to know she was preserving Deacon Island.

SAM: Yeah? How did she know? Tell me. How did she know?

GABE: Everyone in Florida knows that you get the deal you're after. I worked on it. I made a disaster out of it. But you got it going. This is your deal. This is your gift to Hannah, just as you intended. I tell you . . . if all of Florida knew you'd get this done—and they did—surely Hannah knew it too. I promise you, Sam. I promise you. The morning Hannah woke up, that last morning. She knew her dad was going to save Deacon Island. She knew you'd get it done . . . for her. She had to know.

SAM: OK. I've got that much . . . Gabe, did David know you loved him?

GABE: Yes, he knew that. The drugs pulled him far away from me. But not so far that he didn't know I loved him.

SAM: Then you've got something too. You're asking me to take consolation in all this grief and agony. OK, I'm gonna try. And I'll make that work, if I can, for Louise. But you have to find some consolation in what David knew.

GABE: I can try. And maybe the Preserve will help. Hell, maybe I'll walk around in there and think about David. Think especially about those early years when he had both his parents, when he was a happy child.

SAM: OK, Gabe. We're partners again in one more deal, the hardest one. We promise each other that we will not close down our hearts. We will remember the love amid the loss. We will remember that love as we finish our lives.

The End

Postscript to "What We Preserve"

Jews are perpetual outsiders—but not in Jewish Florida. Moreover, Sam and Gabe didn't retire to Florida. As far as we know, they've always lived there, and they've done a lot of big deals. Sam and Gabe aren't merely comfortable in Florida. They think they own the place.

Aristotle, says that a tragic hero should be a man of stature who is good but not pre-eminently good and whose downfall is brought about not by vice or depravity but only by some flaw or error (*Poetics,* 1902 edition). One likely flaw is pride or reckless self-confidence (hubris), which brings about an error in judgment (hamartia). This is what we see in Sam and Gabe. Their objectives are admirable, but the men exhibit overconfidence and even recklessness, especially when Gabe declares that he may need to "play a little rough" with the Florida State legislature. However, as in many tragedies, Sam and Gabe find a spark of redemption and hope— which at least approximates Aristotle's catharsis.

In Scene 4, Gabe, trying to console Sam, suggests that Hannah lives on after her physical death and knows that Deacon Island has been saved. When Sam sharply rejects the idea of an afterlife—which is not prominent in North American Judaism—Gabe offers a scaled-down, entirely secular consolation: Hannah died knowing that her father was going to fulfill her fondest wish. This strategy succeeds, leading to the mutual redemption that we see as the play ends.

Proof of God

A 10-minute play by

David K. Farkas

Version 03-25-22

Setting:

A residential neighborhood in Lubbock, Texas, in the early fall of 1976.

Characters:

David Farkas: A new assistant professor at Texas Tech University. He speaks with a New York City accent.
Pastor Donald Jenkins: David's across-the-street neighbor. He speaks with a West Texas accent.

[Scene 1]

DAVID stands in front of his house watering his lawn with a garden hose. DON strolls across the street to greet him. Optionally, a narrator can state that the play is set in 1976 in Lubbock, Texas.

DON: Hello.

DAVID: Hi.

DON: You and your wife are the new folks on the street. How do you like it so far?

DAVID: Fine. Thank you.

DON: And you're new to Lubbock? To Texas, maybe?

DAVID: Yes.

DON: Well, welcome! I'm Don. Don Jenkins. Pastor Jenkins, actually.

DAVID: I'm Dave. Dave Farkas.

DON: "David," right out of the Bible.

DAVID: Yes.

DON: "Far" "Kiss"?

DAVID: That's Hungarian.

DON: Oh, Hungarian. Hungarians are mostly Catholic. Are you Catholic?

DAVID: No.

DON: What line of work are you in?

DAVID: Well, in two weeks, when the semester starts, I'll be an assistant professor in the English department at Texas Tech.

DON: Everyone here respects Tech. Great school. We all know that. And, of course, there's the Red Raiders. Good chance to win the Southwest Conference this year.

> DAVID nods faintly, suggesting minimal interest. DON turns to DAVID'S automobile parked in the driveway. He's obviously looked at it before.

DON: Interesting automobile. Never seen anything like it.

DAVID: It's a Volvo. It's Swedish.

DON: "VAHL-vah." It would be the Swedish to name a car like that. Their movies are that way too.

> DAVID is initially puzzled. Then he figures it out.

DAVID: It's a "Vole Voe." Has nothing to do with the body of a female.

DON: Oh. Well, that's better. *(Awkward pause.)* David, since we're talking about . . . uh . . . the female body. Two times I've seen your daughter running around here absolutely naked. Susan and I have two boys—six and eight. We'd rather they didn't . . .

DAVID: Oh. OK. Sure. We don't want Eva running around naked either. She's still in diapers, and we definitely want those diapers on her. But it's a lot warmer in Lubbock than what she's used to, and I think sometimes she pulls off the diapers and heads straight out the door—she can reach the handle of the screen door.

DON: I'd appreciate . . .

DAVID: What if we just make sure she keeps her diaper on?

DON: I think she should be wearing a sundress, or a T-shirt, or something on top. When she's outside, I mean.

DAVID: All right. We can do that. Although, on top, she doesn't look any different than your boys. But, sure, we can do that.

DON: May I ask where you and your wife are from? You don't talk anything like the way we do. Your license plate says Minnesota, but I don't think you talk like you're from Minnesota.

DAVID: We moved down here from Minnesota. I was in graduate school at the University of Minnesota, and Jean was editing books for the University of Minnesota Press. But originally we're from the New York City area.

DON nods. DAVID'S answer has confirmed some of DON'S impressions regarding DAVID.

DON: Have you thought about what church you'll be attending? You might consider the Sixth Baptist Church, that's my church. We're a small congregation. Nothing like First Baptist with its five pastors and four associate pastors. At Sixth Baptist, I'm the pastor, and there's Susan helping me. She helps me in so many ways. Everyone at our church is happy to meet new folks. You and your wife would feel at home very quickly.

DAVID: Well, no. Actually, we won't be attending any church. We're Jews.

DON: Real Jews?

DAVID: Yup. We're very real. Both us were born Jewish on both sides of the family.

DON: I've never met a Jewish person before. Of course, I know a lot about Jews from the Bible. And I've seen Jews in Biblical movies. You know, like *Ben Hur*.

DAVID: Sure.

DON: That's a movie both Jews and Christians can enjoy—don't you think? Some day I'm hoping to visit the Holy Land. I expect I'll see a lot of Jews there. *(Pause.)* Just because you're Jewish doesn't mean you're not welcome in our church. In fact, you're very welcome.

DAVID: Thank you. Your church does sound very friendly.

DON: I also have a weekly radio show. Fifteen minutes every Sunday morning starting at 6:30. KLTX, 88.1. Not big-time broadcasting. Just a local station, although the signal reaches all of Lubbock County and even beyond. The station is real good about supporting Christian broadcasting. For the 6:30 slot, they don't hardly charge us at all. I broadcast right from the house. We have a little bit of a studio right in one of the rooms. Just some sound proofing, a mic, and a live link right to the tower. It's sort of a phone line, but with a special box on my end to improve the sound quality.

DAVID: Well, I'm an early riser. Perhaps I'll catch your show.

DON: Always the same format. Every week I provide a new proof for the existence of God.

DAVID: Wow, that sounds difficult. I don't mean to say that proving the existence of God is difficult. But finding a *new* proof every week sounds challenging.

DON: No, not a challenge at all. Generally, I prove the existence of God by citing scripture. But sometimes I draw upon God's manifest presence in the universe, in our daily lives.

DAVID: Sure, like, the Universe is so complex, so beautiful, only a divine being could have created it.

DON: Yes, I have several different proofs based on that general idea.

DAVID: Well, I'll be sure to listen in. Maybe this Sunday.

DON: Actually, David. I have a different idea. I'd like to interview you on the show. Normally, I'm in the studio by myself. But sometimes I have a guest. I'd like *you* to be a guest. Would you be so kind?

DAVID: Well, I don't know . . . I'm still preparing my classes. And I don't think I'm the kind of person your listeners really want to hear talking about religion and God.

DON: Let me be the judge of that. You're not embarrassed about being of the Jewish faith, are you? Embarrassed to talk about it, I mean.

DAVID: No I'm not.

DON: Then why not share a little about the Jewish faith with me and my listeners? Will you do that, David?

DAVID: It's an interesting idea, but I don't think . . .

DON: If the Jewish faith is your spiritual home, your light, then why keep it hidden under a bushel?

DAVID: Whatever my light may be, I've never kept it hidden at all. And that includes my Jewish background.

DON: Then there we have it! How about this Sunday? All you need to do is walk across the street. Just a little before 6:30. I'll have you set up in a minute. David, you're a teacher. In the classroom you share what you know. So share with us, just like you'll do at Tech.

DAVID: All right. I'll explain a little about myself and my wife and our religious backgrounds. But that *won't* amount to a proof of the existence of god.

DON: That's just fine. We can depart from the regular format for something truly special.

DAVID: OK. I'll do it.

[Scene 2]

DON and DAVID sit on two stools. There is a desk microphone between them and a table on which there is some kind of console with dials and switches. DAVID holds a mug of coffee.

DON: Welcome, everyone, to another morning broadcast of Living Faith. I'm Pastor Donald Jenkins of Lubbock's Sixth Baptist Church. Now, I know some of you are listening from your homes, some of you are on your tractors, and some of you are on the highway driving through these parts. But, wherever you are, I hope you will stick with us for 15 minutes of Living Faith. *(Chuckling.)* And, of course, get to church later in the morning. This Sunday is a very special show. I have here with me, right in our studio, David Farkas. He is a member of the Jewish faith. Why don't you say hello to the folks, David?

DAVID: Hello everyone. I'm very pleased to be joining Pastor Jenkins this morning.

DON: I wish all you listeners were right here in the studio with me, so you could see David. He looks like he's right out of the Old Testament. He's tall, bearded, and he has a robe wrapped around him—like you see in all those Bible pictures.

DAVID is startled, then dismayed, then angry. DON grins and continues on creating his visual image of DAVID.

DON: Also, he's wearing Roman sandals. And a Jewish prayer shawl. And a Jewish skull cap, and right on the front of the skull cap, there's a Jewish Star of David. He's like a living image of the Holy Land!

DAVID, ready to leave, begins to stand. But DON, still smiling, puts his arm on DAVID'S shoulder in a restraining gesture. DAVID settles back onto his stool, looking annoyed.

DON: David has agreed to offer us a proof of the existence of God. A Jewish proof. Now Jews do not believe in the Divinity of Our Lord Jesus Christ. You all know that. But they do believe in God. So I'm sure that David will explain to us why people of the Jewish faith believe in God.

DAVID: Well, Pastor. I'm pleased to be part of your show, but I'm not prepared to offer a proof for the existence of God.

DON: Well, David. How do you maintain your Jewish faith, if you don't have a single proof for the existence of God? Perhaps you have not yet found your spiritual home. Perhaps today is the day for you to let Christ into your heart and into your Life. Here we have many, many proofs for the existence of God—the Christian God.

In his irritation, DAVID's mood becomes reckless,

DAVID: Wait, maybe I do have proof. A first-hand experience that proves the existence of God.

DON: A first-hand experience! That's wonderful. That's amazing. What is it, David?

DAVID: My mother-in-law is 83 years old, and she lives on her own. She drives—almost every day—but she has shrunk so much with age that she can barely see over the dashboard. I don't think she sees much of the road at all. She refuses to stop driving. She refuses, even, to sit on a cushion. And, her old Ford Falcon has a malfunction in the steering wheel. When you start turning left—not always, but sometimes—it freezes up. I've driven that car, and when the steering wheel freezes, with all my strength I can't make it budge until it's good and ready. Terribly dangerous. But Ruth says it's just fine, and keeps right on driving that car.

DON: But David, what is your proof for the existence of God?

DAVID: Here it comes: Ruth is a very good person. Very moral, very charitable—and very, very Jewish. She's always kept a Kosher kitchen. Her husband served as president of their synagogue. For years and years, she was the head of the Daughters of Jacob.

DON: So?

DAVID: I can tell you that Yahweh, the Jewish God, definitely exists. Busy as he is, he's watching over Ruth whenever she drives, and he swoops down his hand and lifts Ruth and that Ford Falcon right up into the air just as she's about to get into an accident. There is no other way to explain the fact that Ruth has not yet been in an accident—a major accident. Is that a good enough proof of God for you and your listeners?

DON is surprised by this argument. Then, he gathers his thoughts for an appropriate response.

DON: Well, perhaps it is. God watches even over the sparrow. But, David, why do you say it's the Jewish God that's protecting her? I maintain that it's Jesus Christ. I believe that Jesus Christ, in his infinite mercy, is watching over your mother-in-law even though she has not accepted him as her redeemer.

DAVID: Nope!

DON: On what basis do you reject my argument? How can you say that the Christian God is not looking after your mother-in-law?

DAVID: Well, as I said, I have first-hand proof.

DON: What?

DAVID: Once I was in the car with her. I asked to drive, but she insisted. We were heading into an intersection. She didn't see the stop sign, and she drove straight through, didn't even slow down. A big semi was bearing down hard on us. There was no way for him to stop. And—suddenly—I felt the car lift straight up into the air.

DON: You did?

DAVID: Yes!

DON: But this still doesn't prove the existence of the Jewish God.

DAVID: Wait a moment.

> DAVID picks up the desktop microphone and stands. He addresses the theater audience, which we understand to be the broadcast audience as well.

DAVID: As we went up into the air, I looked out the window. And I saw God. He was maybe the size of a 10-story building. He was tall, bearded. He looked a lot like me actually. He was wearing a robe—like in all those Bible pictures. And, he wore Roman sandals. Also, he was wearing a Jewish prayer shawl and a Jewish skull cap with a Star of David.

> DON is initially flummoxed, but then finds a response. He will not be defeated by a guest on his own radio show.

DON: Well, thank you, David. Folks, that was David, our Jewish guest on this week's Living Faith radio show. David's testimony is a reminder to all of us that those who do not follow the teachings of Christ are subject to delusions and false visions. I do not speak ill of this man. He is a neighbor and a friend. But I do hope—I pray—that he will proceed in his spiritual journey from the dark shadows to the light. So, here we conclude today's very special broadcast of the Living Faith radio show!

DON flicks a switch on the console, relaxes, and turns to DAVID.

DON: Well, thank you for being on my show this morning. I hope nothing offended or upset you.

DAVID: I'm surprised, but not upset. This is your show, and the listeners are your people. But you did tell an outrageous lie about how I looked and dressed. I wasn't expecting that.

DON: Yes, yes. But, you know, Christian broadcasting does include an element of entertainment. There wasn't anything bad in what I said. I just wanted my listeners to have a strong visual image of Jews, the People of the Old Testament. And David, I think you also told an untruth. You didn't actually see Jehovah lifting you up in the air—did you?

DAVID: No, I never saw Yahweh. I was bringing my own element of entertainment to Christian broadcasting.

DON: So, perhaps this is where we should leave it. A little bit of colorful exaggeration on both sides. If you're not unhappy with what happened, I'm certainly not unhappy. This will be one of my most memorable shows. Folks will be talking about it for a long time . . . David, I hope we can be neighbors and friends. And talk some more about religion.

DAVID: One more thing I want to mention: We agreed that you'd set aside your proof of God format for my interview, and then you blind-sided me.

DON: When you accepted my invitation to be on the show, we agreed that you didn't want to hide your light under a bushel. *(Chuckling.)* I just gave you the opportunity to let your light shine. And it sure did shine.

DAVID: That light's gonna keep on shining. Jean and I have been in Lubbock just over a week, and there've been several cultural collisions already. I'm getting the idea that there will be more—religion, politics, child-rearing. The racism that flourishes around here.

DON: Are you sorry you moved to West Texas?

DAVID: No, I think Jean and I can be ourselves. Not shy away from expressing our values—and still get along in Lubbock.

DON: I think so too. I want you to feel at home, despite the differences.

DAVID: Thank you, Don.

DON: You know, things here are starting to change. We treat our Mexican and Negro people better now. And because of Texas Tech, we have some Chinese and even Pakistanian people here.

DAVID: Well, I'm glad to do my little bit to bring some more diversity and new thinking to West Texas.

DON: I have an idea for something new. You and your wife can be the first Jewish family at the Sixth Baptist Church.

DAVID: That's not going to happen. But for sure we can be good neighbors and friends. I'll exchange viewpoints with you any time. And I will do my very best to keep our daughter from running around naked on our front lawn.

The End

Postscript to "Proof of God"

Jean and I did not encounter any overt anti-Semitism during our two years in Lubbock. Racism directed toward Blacks, Latinx, Asians, and Native Americans was a very different story. But Jews, it seemed, were too scarce and too unfamiliar—an oddity, like druids. And because Lubbock was such a Christian city, Jews were strongly associated with the Old Testament. Hence, there was great curiosity, at least on the part of educated Lubbockites, about Jews, including Jewish food. Realizing this, Jean and I began inviting folks to our house for a breakfast of blintzes. This invitation was a hot ticket in Lubbock.

Not that there wasn't much in Lubbock that might offend a Jew. High-school sports events and civic meetings frequently (and illegally) began with an invocation that made reference to Jesus Christ. On one occasion Jean was invited to a luncheon at the home of a Lubbock woman on whose door was a cute little ceramic plaque reading, "If you have a smile on your face and Christ in your heart, you are welcome here." Jean ignored the inscription and rang the doorbell.

I routinely and good naturedly answered odd questions. Having learned that I was a Jew, the chairman of the Texas Tech Petroleum Engineering Department asked me "How can you be a Jew? Judaism has no database." "What?" "If you believe in the literal truth of the Bible, your religion has a database." More than once I was asked if I was a Sadducee or a Pharisee. I had no objection to teaching the good people of Lubbock a little about modern-day Judaism.

The play begins factually. However, our neighbor (whom I call "Don") never invited me to appear on his radio show. When Don had visitors (many of whom were ministers and their wives), he would eagerly take them across the street so they could meet me and ask questions about Judaism. They tended to ignore Jean because she was female. Most of these folks had not previously met a Jew.

Don never gave up on trying to convert me to Christianity. But his arguments were almost always predicated on the idea that I believed in God—but the wrong God. He had trouble grasping the idea that I might not wholeheartedly believe in a divine being who ruled heaven and earth.

Sally from the Bronx

A 10-minute play by

David K. Farkas

Characters:

Narrator/Comedian/Rattlesnake/Rabbi: Any gender.
Sally Silberman Farkas (1914–2009): Appears as an apparition on the day of her funeral.
David Farkas: Her older son, middle aged.
Mitchell Farkas: Her younger son, middle aged.

Setting:

DAVID and MITCHELL, wearing jackets and ties, yarmulkes, and tallits (prayer shawls) are standing by the open grave of their mother SALLY FARKAS. The NARRATOR, in a jacket and tie, stands near them. SALLY stands apart but is listening.

✳✳✳

NARRATOR: David and Mitchell Farkas are part of the group of mourners by the newly dug grave of their mother, Sally Silberman Farkas, at the Mt. Ararat Cemetery, Farmington, Long Island, 2009.

DAVID: (*Addressing the entire, largely unseen group.*) My mother was a complex person. I won't try to characterize her. Instead, I'll tell three brief stories. We've all been sharing stories about Sally today, and I hope we keep doing so.

    SALLY approaches DAVID and the group.

NARRATOR: First Graveside Story: The White Shirt.

DAVID: A few years back when I was visiting Sally, she surprised me with a question.

SALLY: Do you have a plain white shirt for my funeral?

DAVID: Why are we talking about your funeral?

SALLY: I asked you a question: Do you have a plain white shirt?

DAVID: I have a light blue one, I think.

SALLY: When you get back to Seattle, you go buy a plain white shirt for my funeral. You can't be an embarrassment.

DAVID: Well, Sally. *(Pointing to his chest.)* Here's the plain white shirt.

NARRATOR: Second Graveside Story: Social Justice.

DAVID: In New Jersey we had a cleaning lady, Cleo, who worked for our family for many years. Sally and Cleo spent a lot of time together, and I think Cleo was actually Sally's closest friend. It got to bother Sally that Cleo didn't have Social Security. Sally thought about the other cleaning ladies as well. She began to talk to the housewives in Rolling Hills, our upscale development. Those women were not happy at the thought of paying more money each week to cover Social Security, and Sally was never inclined to rock the boat and create problems with her neighbors and friends. But this needed to be done, and Sally persisted. After a few months, Cleo and all the other cleaning ladies who got off the bus from the poor black neighborhoods of Paterson to clean homes in Rolling Hills were enrolled in Social Security.

MITCHELL: *(Addressing the audience.)* Well, yes, that's all true and very admirable. But Mother *did* have her prejudices. When Dave and I were boys, if we were grocery shopping with Sally, and if we showed an interest in anything on the shelves that Sally did not like, she had the same answer.

SALLY: *(Sharply.)* That's what the Polish women buy!

NARRATOR: Third Graveside Story: Worms in the Fridge.

DAVID: In their later years, Sally and Al moved to Florida.

MITCHELL: I'm not sure they even wanted to *be* in Florida, but, as the Jewish comedian said . . .

NARRATOR AS COMEDIAN: *(With a comically strong New York City accent.)* My parents retired to Florida. They didn't want to go. But, you know. It's the law!

MITCHELL: Her three sisters were already living . . .

SALLY: Mitchell! I've had enough of your interruptions. This is my funeral service. David, tell the story about the worms. It's a nice story. I *like* it.

DAVID: Yes, Mother. *(Turns to audience.)* Al was bored by his routine in Florida. I thought that he might like to try fishing in the local lakes. So, during my next visit, I bought a rod, reel, tackle box, and everything else— including a dozen nightcrawlers. We did a little fishing, and it worked out well . . . When we got back to the house, I realized we had a big problem. I explained to Sally that the only way the nightcrawlers would stay alive was in the refrigerator.

> A small table has appeared just behind SALLY. From the table (or through some stage trick), she picks up the container of nightcrawlers. It is one of those round, quart-size cardboard containers used for take-out food. Moist peat moss can be seen protruding slightly through the many sizable holes that were poked through the container at the bait shop. Sally examines the container with disgust.

DAVID: With dread, Sally envisioned nightcrawlers roaming through her refrigerator. But she didn't say a word.

> With disgust, but also resignation, she opens an imaginary refrigerator door, finds a place for the container, and closes the refrigerator door.

DAVID: She loved Al totally. She loved Al enough to keep worms in her fridge—that's totally. So, those are my three brief stories about Sally.

SALLY: Why not tell another one? Come on. People are interested.

DAVID: OK, Muth-ther. This is your day.

> MITCHELL steps forward to interrupt.

MITCHELL: Even when we were very young, Sally hated for us to call her "Mommy" or even "Mom." She was always *(Adopting a deep, formal voice and a British accent.)* . . . Muth-ther

SALLY scowls. MITCHELL steps back.

NARRATOR: Fourth Graveside Story: I'll die in New York.

DAVID: One summer, we took a long vacation out West to visit the national parks. But there was an ominous aspect to this trip. Sally had always suffered from asthma, and it seemed to be getting worse. The doctor had recommended moving to Arizona. So, after seeing the Grand Canyon, we were now driving south through flat, parched scrublands toward Phoenix, our prospective new home. No one was talking much. My father would have to start all over in business. Mitchell and I had no desire to leave everyone and everything we knew. The hours went by. It got drier and drier, more parched and more barren. Sally suddenly cried out.

SALLY: Turn the car around, honey. I'll die in New York!

DAVID: Not another word was spoken. Al took the next exit, and we headed back north. Her asthma somehow got better back home in New Jersey. It was no surprise that Sally said "die in *New York*." New Jersey, Florida—wherever she might live, Sally Silberman was most definitely Sally from the Bronx.

MITCHELL: While Sally and Al were living in Florida, Sally suffered a moderate stroke. Sally was a good bridge player, and after she recovered, she was afraid she'd lost something mentally, and she refused to play. One morning, a friend from Sally's bridge group phoned, "Sally. I'm coming to get you for bridge. In half an hour. You better have some clothes on." Sally won seven dollars that day. To her, it was like millions. She started playing bridge again.

NARRATOR AS RATTLESNAKE: Hsssss. *(Shakes a child's rattle.)* I'm a rattlesnake. I live in one of the few remaining pine woods in Jewish Florida.

DAVID: Who invited *you*?

NARRATOR AS RATTLESNAKE: *(Undeterred.)* These old Jews from New York are very annoying. One sunny morning, Sally Farkas spotted me lounging in her driveway. I like the warm macadam. Having no fear or even minimal respect for my species, she grabbed me right behind my head with her barbecue tongs. What chutzpah! I struggled furiously, but she had me pretty good. She released me in the weeds where her backyard borders a drainage canal . . . My buddy tells a different story. One chilly morning he's lounging on the *Sunday New York Times*, when Al Farkas, wearing a bathrobe and bedroom slippers, opens the front door, takes a look, kicks my buddy right off the warm newspaper, picks up the paper, and takes it into the house. My buddy says he'd rather have been shot dead by a real Florida man than be humiliated like that.

DAVID: Thank you for sharing, but that will be enough. You may return to South Florida.

The NARRATOR AS RATTLESNAKE turns as if to leave, but loops around, and returns as the NARRATOR.

MITCHELL: After Al died, Sally resented any woman who still had a husband. She said it like this:

SALLY: They have a heart attack. The ambulance comes. You think it's over. *(Full of indignation.)* But they come *back!*

DAVID: Here's a final story—very brief. Although Sally never graduated from high school, she was—in that Jewish way—quite the rhetorician. She certainly got the better of me on this one.

DAVID: *(Pretending to hold an old landline phone.)* Hello, Muth-her How are you?

SALLY: *(Very loud and emphatic.)* How could I be?

DAVID raises his hands high in exasperation.

NARRATOR: It was checkmate in one move.

DAVID: Now all that restless energy is stilled, and Sally will finally lie, once again, alongside her husband.

The NARRATOR dons a tallit, places a yarmulke on their head, and becomes a rabbi.

NARRATOR AS RABBI: We will now recite the Mourner's Kaddish.

The End

Postscript to "Sally from the Bronx"

Sally was hyper-verbal. She had largely erased her Jewish accent, but a bit of Yiddish undergirded her syntax. She was terse, vivid, and sharp-tongued to the point of cruelty. I used to say that Sally was a "gun turret of ridicule." Most people hold a set of values from which they ridicule people with different values. Sally would adopt whatever value system was convenient. If Sally heard that one of her friends had encouraged her daughter-in-law to have a "nose job," Sally would offer a harsh assessment of that woman: "What, she wants a daughter-in-law with a button nose like a shiksa?" But Sally never let up on Jean's Jewish nose. "Mick Jagger had a nose job, so why won't you?" Jean had decidedly mixed feelings toward my mother and did not look forward to our visits.

Formulating an argument on any public issue was for men to do. But occasionally Sally would offer a one- or two-sentence remark. She did not like gay people ("homosexuals," she would have said), but she did not like the Republicans who attacked homosexuals. After Pat Buchanan's notorious "culture wars" speech at the Republican National Convention of 1992 (when George H. W. Bush was nominated for a second term), Sally commented, "Republicans spend much too much time worrying about what people do with their penises."

The stay-at-home wife

When I was a young boy, I often heard Sally express great pride that her husband earned enough that she didn't have to work. Much later, when "Women's Lib" appeared, Sally was hostile to the whole thing, "Women have it so good now. We don't go off to work in the morning. We shouldn't rock the boat." Of course, she was thinking about the income brackets in which wives were not economically compelled to work.

Sally never recognized the price she paid for her ideas about social standing. There was so much idleness in her life. Sally and her three sisters were bred for marriage to upwardly mobile Jewish men. All four girls were smart, good-looking and dressed fashionably, and all four married successful Jewish men.

After completing secretarial school, Sally worked for a Jewish-owned fabric business. This is what you did until you married. Her sister Anne got a similar job at another firm. Both women, however, found themselves in management roles when many of the men who ran the businesses went off to war in 1941.

After the war, these women—and many, many more—readily surrendered their jobs to the returning men. Sally's sister Florence (whose original first name was "Fruma") married my Uncle Joe. Sally (who had once been "Sadie") married Al, just a year after he returned from the South Pacific. Then began about 60 years of idleness. Sally was a disengaged mother for the 20 years that Mitchell and I were growing up. Apart from a weekly bridge or mahjong game and some socializing on Saturday nights, how did she pass the hours? She bought groceries and prepared dinner, but most of the house-cleaning was done by Cleo. Sally wasn't much for soap operas or television, and she wasn't much for reading. During her decades of widowhood, she didn't even have Al in the house with her. How did she pass the hours?

I recall with amazement that in 1957 or 1958, Sally, now living in New Jersey, was an officer for the local chapter of the Jewish philanthropic organization ORT (Organization for Rehabilitation through Training). I remember her at the kitchen table confidently rehearsing a luncheon address she would give to an audience of dozens of people. She intoned, "We will make the Negev bloom!" To do this kind of thing requires ability and self-confidence, but somehow Sally's ORT work gradually petered out, and she never did any volunteer work or spoke a word in any public setting for the rest of her life. Perhaps Sally became such a fierce-tongued commentator on everything around her at least in part because of all that untapped energy and ability.

Sunday Walk in North Creek Park

A 10-minute play by

David K. Farkas

Characters:

Narrator
Dan: A man in his mid-70s.
Jenn: His wife, in her mid-70s.
T-shirt Woman: A woman in her mid-70s.
T-shirt Man: A man in his mid-70s.
Mother: A woman in her 30s.
Daughter: About 6 years old.
Father: A man in his 30s.
Boy 1: Between 6 and 9 years old.
Boy 2: Between 6 and 9 years old.

Suggested minimum casting:

- Dan
- Jenn/Boy 2
- Narrator/T-shirt Man/Daughter (in a comic falsetto)/Father
- T-shirt Woman/Mother/Boy 1

Setting and Staging:

There is no set. However, the staging should reinforce the idea that JENN and DAN are walking on a boardwalk. The stage directions assume an unrealistically comic staging in which adult actors double as the children. The play can also be staged naturalistically with actual child actors.

✳✳✳

NARRATOR: On a pleasant summer morning, Dan and Jenn are strolling on the wooden boardwalk that runs through North Creek Park. There is swampy ground on both sides of the boardwalk. Wetland grasses grow in profusion. Birds are chirping.

The NARRATOR exits. JENN and DAN enter.

JENN: You know that Jonah and Hazel will be at our house next weekend. I don't want them watching a lot of Pink Panther videos. We need to plan out some activities.

DAN: Sure. Why not take them up here? They'd like it. Have we taken them here before?

JENN: I don't think so.

DAN: There! We have part of the weekend planned out already.

JENN: OK . . . I really like this place. It's great that they preserved such a big area with all the development taking place around here.

DAN: Yes. But you can bet the County got the land easily enough. No one could ever build anything on this swamp.

They continue on their walk.

JENN: Did you hear that Idaho wants to annex Eastern Oregon and Eastern Washington? That would give them more Republican votes in Congress.

They slow down and then stop as they argue.

DAN: Not likely to happen. Anyway, it's five counties in Eastern Oregon that told the Oregon legislature they want to secede and join Idaho. They say they don't get listened to in Salem. Hardly anybody even lives in those five counties. It's like emp-tee out there.

JENN: No, Idaho said they wanted to annex Eastern Oregon *and* Eastern Washington.

DAN: Nooo.

JENN: Yes. That's what Idaho said. And it can be done. States can vote to change their borders.

DAN: When you say "Idaho said," who do you mean? Was some law passed? Something the state legislature did officially? Or did a handful of crazies at the county level say all this? Anyway, there's been talk about "The Inland Empire" for decades.

JENN: Never mind. Sorry I brought it up. I just thought you'd want to know about this.

DAN: I wasn't going to learn anything anyway. Your facts are too mixed up.

JENN: *(With bitter sarcasm.)* Thank you.

They walk on in irritated silence. The NARRATOR enters.

NARRATOR: The day is not going well! Now Dan and Jenn encounter another elderly couple who are wearing identical black T-shirts that recall the "Twilight Zone," a science-fiction TV show from the early 60s.

The NARRATOR slips on a "Twilight Zone" T-shirt and becomes T-SHIRT Man. T-SHIRT Woman enters and joins her husband. (The two T-shirts need be no more than cardboard cutouts with armholes.)

DAN: *(Cheerfully.)* You folks must really like "The Twilight Zone"!

T-SHIRT MAN: Well, yes. I remember that show. I liked it.

DAN: That was like 60 years ago. Not many of us left. Remember the one where the aliens get the people in a town to kill each other, just by controlling the street lights?

T-SHIRT WOMAN: *(Pointing to her chest.)* Actually, these are not "Twilight Zone" T-shirts. They're from a casino named "Z Twilight Zone." They use the letter Z instead of "The."

DAN: Oh. I didn't notice the Z. That's odd.

T-SHIRT WOMAN: Ben and I don't even go to casinos. We have friends who went there. They bought themselves T-shirts, but the T-shirts didn't fit, so they gave them to us.

JENN: Well, it's been nice chatting with you.

DAN: *(Cheerfully.)* Enjoy your day in matching T-shirts.

T-SHIRT MAN: We always wear matching T-shirts when we go out together. We have a lot of them.

DAN: Why do you wear matching T-shirts?

T-SHIRT MAN: We wear them so if we get separated, like at the mall, we can look at our T-shirt and know what the other one is wearing.

DAN: Sure, makes total sense. Without the matching T-shirt, you might never find her. "Bye, bye, wife!" You might wander around in that mall forever.

T-SHIRT WOMAN: *(Angry.)* What are you implying? Are you insulting my husband's intelligence? Maybe your own brain isn't in such good working order.

DAN: I'm sorry. I just wanted to understand why you wear matching T-shirts. Then I joked a little bit. I didn't mean to suggest anything about intelligence.

T-SHIRT WOMAN: *(More angry.)* Well, your little joke was rude. And making fun of memory loss is a form of bigotry! *(To husband.)* Let's go, Dear.

She takes her husband by the arm. They exit.

DAN: Wow! That didn't go well.

JENN: It never does when you just start talking to people.

DAN and JENN continue strolling down the boardwalk. Their mood is chilly at best. The T-SHIRT WOMAN enters as the MOTHER. The NARRATOR, kneeling (shins on the ground) enters as the DAUGHTER. DAN and JENN are walking just behind the MOTHER and DAUGHTER.

DAUGHTER: *(With trepidation.)* Are there lions here?

MOTHER: *(Gesturing out toward the grasslands.)* No, Bethany. There are no lions here. Just small animals. Nice animals. All the lions live in the jungle, and that's far away.

DAUGHTER: OK, Mommy.

DAN bends his head close to Bethany's and gives a big, fierce lion roar.

DAN: AAAARRHHHHH!

DAUGHTER: *(Sobbing and half-choking.)* Uh! Oh! Oh! Uh! Oh!

DAN recoils in horror. The MOTHER, after recovering herself, wheels around in rage.

DAUGHTER: Uh! Uh! Oh! Oh! Uh! Oh!

MOTHER: How dare you! Look what you've done!

DAUGHTER: Uh! Oh! Oh! Uh! Oh! Uh!

DAN: I'm sorry. I thought it would be . . .

DAUGHTER: Uh! Oh! Oh! Uh! Oh! Uh!

MOTHER: What's *wrong* with you?

DAUGHTER: Uh! Oh! Oh! Uh! Oh! Uh!

DAN: . . . a fun thing.

JENN: We're very sorry. He didn't mean to upset your daughter.

MOTHER: You need to keep him under control. Do you understand me?

JENN: Yes. And I'm not arguing.

MOTHER: Let's go, Bethany. There are no lions here. Just stupid men!

The MOTHER and DAUGHTER exit. JENN is furious. She walks ahead of DAN and eventually exits. DAN walks on alone, looking very dejected. The T-SHIRT MAN enters as the FATHER. He is enthusiastically staring into the water just beyond the edge of the boardwalk. The T-SHIRT WOMAN, with clothing items that suggest a boy, enters kneeling (shins on the ground). She is now BOY 1, who is looking into the water with excitement. JENN, with clothing items that suggest a boy, enters kneeling (shins on the ground). She is now BOY 2, who is also looking into the water with excitement. DAN approaches the FATHER with an open, eager manner. He obviously wants to know what's going on.

FATHER: *(Addressing DAN cheerfully and pointing.)* There's a frog down there. Right in that clump of weeds.

DAN: Yes, I see!

BOY 1 Daddy, catch the frog for us! Daddy, please catch the frog.

FATHER: No, no. We'll leave that frog alone. We don't want to hurt him.

BOY 2 We won't hurt him. *Please* catch the frog. We want to see him close up.

FATHER: No, I'm not going after that frog.

DAN: It wouldn't be hard to catch him. And if you're careful you won't hurt him.

FATHER: *(Icily.)* Thank . . . you.

BOY 1 and **BOY 2:** Please. Please catch the frog!

DAN: I'll be *happy* to do it for you. I've caught frogs for my grandkids. You just need to slide your hand . . .

FATHER: *(Angrily.)* Why don't you go find *your* grandchildren and catch them a frog? I'm handling things here.

DAN: *(Very unhappy and apologetic.)* Uh . . . OK. Have a great day.

> DAN walks on while the FATHER, BOY 1, and BOY 2 make quick, inconspicuous exits. JENN (who was BOY 2) now appears at the far end of the boardwalk. She is looking back at DAN with a baleful look and a hand on her hip. Soon DAN catches up with JENN.

JENN: What happened down there?!

DAN: Nothing. Just a man showing his kids a frog.

JENN: No. More happened than that. What did you do?

DAN: I didn't do anything. I just . . . talked to them for a little while.

JENN: *(Not believing DAN.)* We're done here. I'm taking you home.

DAN: But . . . there's a whole 'nother part to the boardwalk. It's really nice. It leads to a little pond.

JENN: I've had it with you. We're going home.

DAN: That's really not necessary.

JENN: You'd better keep up with me. When I get to the parking lot, I'm driving home. If you're not with me, you can walk home. Or else live in North Creek Park.

> JENN walks quickly back to the start of the boardwalk. DAN follows with a very unhappy look on his face. An actor or stagehand has entered and has placed what will serve for a metal sign on a post. It's a map of North Creek Park and the surrounding streets. (The audience does not need a detailed look at the sign.) DAN is eager to make conversation.

DAN: Did you notice? This map is not useful.

JENN: What do you mean?

DAN: Well, the map's upside down. It shows the parking lot at the wrong end of the boardwalk. People are definitely going to get confused.

JENN: No. It's a normal map. Up is north. People understand that. See, there's even a legend that makes everything clear. You obviously never learned to read a map. Must have been one of those days in elementary school when you daydreamed about building your bomb.

DAN: *(Trying desperately to be appeasing and cute.)* Yes. You're right. I remember that day. The teacher said to us, "Today we're going to learn how to read maps." I said to myself, "Should I learn to read maps or work on my bomb?"

> DAN pantomimes turning a screw and otherwise putting the finishing touches on a bomb.

DAN: I guess I made the wrong choice.

JENN: Do *not* tell Jonah and Hazel that you sat in your seat ignoring your teacher, working on an imaginary bomb that would blow up the school.

DAN: I'd *never* say anything like that to Jonah and Hazel.

JENN: Of course you would. In fact, you *will*. The moment will come. You'll have that impulse, and this will be one more of your crazy stories.

DAN: I tell you I'd never say anything like that to Jonah and Hazel. But it *would* make a good story. You know . . . you didn't do me a favor with the idea that my bomb might make for a fun story. Now I'm going to have to *resist* telling Jonah and Hazel. It won't be easy.

JENN: God! Worse and worse.

DAN: No, not worse. Not at all. Being tempted and resisting is a virtue.

JENN: I'm not interested in your arguments, your distinctions. I can't stand living with a screwy old pedant who annoys people everywhere he goes. Look what you've made of what *could* have been a nice walk in the park!

DAN wheels around and takes big steps back toward the boardwalk.

JENN: What are you doing?

Dan turns back to face JENN.

DAN: Goodbye! Idon't seem to be succeeding with the human race. I think I'll try my luck living in the muck with the frogs.

DAN turns again and takes a step or two back toward the boardwalk. He throws his arms in the air as if to say goodbye to the human race.

JENN: Stop. Come back here. Leave the frogs in peace.

DAN turns again to address JENN.

DAN: No. I'm a walking disaster. I'm best off living with the frogs. Or maybe I'll be a solitary muck creature.

DAN turns once more toward the boardwalk.

JENN: Stop it! Come back here. You're ridiculous, but not much worse than that. Come back here, Muck Man! I love you.

DAN turns apprehensively to face JENN, whose manner suggests forgiveness.

The End

Postscript to "Sunday Walk in North Creek Park"

"Sunday Walk in North Creek Park" makes no mention of Jews or Judaism. But the main character—who (alas!) is me—is both a schlemiel (Pinsker, 1971) and an Arguing Jew (Huberman, 2018) of the worst sort. As a schlemiel, Dan is well meaning and eager to please. He is also curious about other people. But, being a schlemiel, his social ineptitude turns his interactions with others into minor disasters (Pinsker, 1971). Furthermore, Dan misuses his instinct for arguing. When Jenn, Dan's wife, expresses anxiety about Republican political power, Dan subjects his wife's offhand remark to unnecessary scrutiny. Then he turns combative, arrogant, and insulting.

With the father and his two sons, Dan pushes much too hard on the idea that the frog can and should be caught. In the manner of a schlemiel, he never knows when enough is enough.

As the play ends, Dan, trying to repair a bad situation, opens up a conversational gambit—the inadequacy of the map. But now Jenn has become aggressive. She stridently insists that she's right about the map, and she mockingly attributes his misinterpretation to Dan's grade-school bomb-making fantasy.

Dan has a good option for defusing the situation. He need only promise not to tell their grandchildren about his bomb-making fantasy. But Dan causes trouble for himself one more time. First, he blames Jenn for giving him the thought that the bomb might become a good story. Then, he reaches into Jewish ethical thinking (recall the mini-essay "Jewish Ethical Traditions" in the postscript to "The Expulsion from Eden") to pull out the unnecessary and exasperating argument that he should now be regarded as virtuous. With this, the situation reaches rock bottom:

> **JENN:** I'm not interested in your arguments, your distinctions. I can't stand living with a screwy old pedant who annoys people everywhere he goes.

In response, Dan descends into theatrical self-pity, declaring he will now join the frogs in the swamp. Jenn, however, summons up tenderness and offers forgiveness. She is a loving wife, so what else is there for her to do?

Almost all of this play is a near-verbatim transcription of a dreadful Sunday walk that Jean and I took in North Creek Park, north of Seattle. I did, however, restrain my impulse to roar at the little girl who was afraid of lions. So—thankfully—that much of the play is fiction.

Perspective

A 10-minute play by

David K. Farkas

Characters:

Walter R. Warner: A corporate executive but also a serious watercolorist.
Morris Rifkin: A working-class Jew. His clothes are scruffy.

Setting:

At a beachfront park on the New Jersey coast, Walter Warner has set up a professional-looking easel and is working on a watercolor painting. Near the easel is a small folding table and a large pail. He is working intently on his watercolor, painting with careful, delicate strokes. We do not see the painting. Morris Rifkin walks up quietly and observes. Mr. Warner notices Morris but chooses not to acknowledge him. After a short while, Mr. Warner begins to shift his weight back and forth in order to view his painting from slightly different angles. He appears dissatisfied. Then, he takes the sheet of paper from the easel and is about to rip it up. Presumably, the torn pieces will go into the pail.

Production note:

It is important to stage the play so that the easel and painting do not block the audience's view of Warner and Rifk
in. Therefore, if an appropriate painting is available, the painting, resting on the easel, can face the audience. Morris and Mr. Warner, standing downstage of the easel, will also face the audience but can turn upstage in order to attend to the painting when necessary. The

changes to the painting that Warner makes are imagined. In a production in which no painting is available, Warner and Rifkin can face downstage and look at and point to an imagined painting on an imagined easel.

✳✳✳

MORRIS: Wait! What are you doing?

MR. WARNER: It's not coming out right.

MORRIS: I like it.

MR. WARNER: That's because you're not a trained artist.

MORRIS: It kinda looks finished. It can't be fixed?

MR. WARNER: No. Sometimes it just happens this way.

MORRIS: Then let me have it. Since I'm not a trained artist, I'll enjoy it. My wife too.

MR. WARNER: Sorry, can't do that.

MORRIS: We've never owned any kind of original art. Actually, there isn't much of anything up on our walls.

MR. WARNER: You can buy prints for very little money.

MORRIS: I guess. But Manawontic Beach is kind of special for us. We live close by. We've been coming down here since before we were married. What about you?

MR. WARNER: First time here.

MORRIS: Beautiful isn't it?

MR. WARNER: It's OK.

MORRIS: So, can I have the painting? I mean . . . you were just about to rip it up.

MR. WARNER: I'm sorry. But no. I can't compromise my art. The world will not see a Walter R. Warner painting that is not up to my standards. I don't make my living as an artist—that's tough to do. But I'm classically trained.

MORRIS: Well, if you're "classically trained" and do such great work, then your "not-quite-good-enough" painting should be fine for Rachel and me.

MR. WARNER: No, can't do it.

MORRIS: Don't you think that's kind of selfish? Don't artists spread beauty all around them? Make people happy?

MR. WARNER: As soon as serious artists begin to just "make people happy," art is degraded. These days our movies are based on comic books. Once there was Ingmar Bergman. Now it's all made for "the mass market," the "popular taste."

MORRIS: "Popular taste." That's Rachel and me. Making art for people like us is a crime?

MR. WARNER: Let me point out to you that I was just painting quietly, minding my own business. I can't be responsible if you don't like my ideas. You're the one who started arguing with me.

MORRIS: I come from an arguing background.

MR. WARNER looks closely at MORRIS.

MR WARNER: Are you an attorney who dresses down on weekends?

MORRIS: I'm a Jew. That's my arguing background. I wish I'd become a lawyer. Rachel and I would be living better. I just never had the opportunity to get an education. So I drive a bus for Metro.

MR WARNER: Well, you would have been a good lawyer. Or an art critic. Maybe there is something to be said for "just spreading joy," appealing to the popular taste. I can't speak for all artists. But nothing but my best work will be signed "W. R. Warner."

MORRIS: Then don't sign it. No one will know who painted it. Rachel and I won't tell. We'll probably forget your name anyway. Or sign any name. Sign it "Morris Rifkin." That's me. Or sign it "Rachel and Morris Rifkin," like we both painted it.

MR. WARNER: That's ridiculous.

MORRIS: No more ridiculous than ripping up a painting that people would enjoy.

MR. WARNER: *(Annoyed.)* OK. OK. You can have the painting. I'll leave it unsigned.

MORRIS: Thank you so much Mr. Warren.

MR. WARNER: "Warner."

MORRIS: I'm not stupid. I know your name is "Warner." I'm disconnecting you from this painting that you're ashamed of.

MR. WARNER: *(Annoyed.)* Stop already! I said you can have the painting.

> MR. WARNER hands over the painting. MORRIS examines it admiringly, then with a more critical eye.

MORRIS: Can you add one more bird? That would make the painting a little better. *(Pointing.)* Right here.

MR. WARNER: Another bird? You can improve my painting . . . Your name is . . . Sorry, I forgot.

MORRIS: "Morris."

MR. WARNER: OK, Morris. Another bird. I've never done anything like this before.

> MR. WARNER takes back the painting, places it on his easel, and adds another bird.

MORRIS: MR. Warner. See, I remember your name. How about a dog running on the beach?

MR. WARNER: A dog doesn't fit the painting.

MORRIS: But you don't even like the painting. I think a dog would be great. So would Rachel. She loves dogs. So, how about a dog? A spaniel. *(Pointing.)* Right about here.

MR. WARNER: Adding a dog is not a simple thing like adding a bird.

MORRIS: Of course. I understand. Even in the classically trained art world money plays a role. Rachel's birthday is in two weeks.

> MORRIS reaches into his pants pocket.

MORRIS: I'll pay you twenty dollars for the dog.

> He pulls out his wallet and starts fishing for a bill.

MR. WARNER: I don't want your money. I'm a senior vice president at MetLife. Twenty dollars is an inconsequential sum of money to me.

MORRIS: Well, it's not inconsequential to *me*. And I'm willing to pay you.

MR. WARNER: OK. OK. Please put your wallet away. I'll paint the dog. I'll paint anything you want!

MORRIS: Just a dog. I don't want to impose.

> MORRIS puts the bill back in the wallet and puts the wallet back in his pants. MR. WARNER turns his attention to the painting. Both men freeze to suggest the passing of a small amount of time. Then, with MORRIS still frozen, MR. WARNER unfreezes and paints with an air of satisfaction, occasionally turning his attention to MORRIS. Then, he stops painting and MORRIS unfreezes.

MR. WARNER: OK. Morris, how do you like your dog?

> MORRIS examines the painting.

MORRIS: It's terrific. The whole painting is terrific. I'm glad it's nice and big.

MR. WARNER: You know, Morris. It's been . . . interesting. Talking to you. Even adding the dog. Maybe I'm coming to see art just a little differently.

MORRIS: You think the dog makes the painting better?

MR. WARNER: No. Definitely not! . . . I'm seeing painting . . . art in general . . . differently. What it's all about. What it's for. There may be particular reasons, particular occasions, when it's OK to paint for the popular taste. To spread a little joy if I can. To forget about my training and connect as directly as I can with other people. *(Uttered very thoughtfully.)* I haven't done as much of that in my life as I should have. Morris, I'd like to have your painting properly framed. With my signature.

MORRIS: Framed! Thank you.

MR. WARNER: When it comes back from the frame shop, I'd like to come by your house and meet Rachel.

MORRIS: Sure, she'd like that . . . Mr. Warner.

MR. WARNER: Call me, "Walt."

MORRIS: Walt, do you think you can get the painting back from the frame shop before the 23rd? That's Rachel's birthday.

MR. WARNER: I will make sure that happens. We definitely don't want to miss Rachel's birthday. Morris, I've won some major juried competitions over the years. But I think this is my truly special painting. The one that made me think differently about my life.

MORRIS: Since we're talking about changes, maybe I didn't need to come on quite so strong as I did. Like you said, you were just minding your own business. You didn't owe me anything.

MR. WARNER: You were . . . OK.

MORRIS: It worked out well today, but it doesn't always . . . Rachel could tell you a few stories.

MR. WARNER: Well, I hope she does. And it will be a great thing if you improve your approach to life, just as I plan to.

MORRIS: Yes, it's never too late to start doing things better.

MR. WARNER: *(Laughing.)* Maybe this was the day for us both to change our perspectives.

The End

Postscript to "Perspective"

In my private playwriting vocabulary, when a Jewish character appears with a WASP (white Anglo-Saxon Protestant), the WASP is likely to carry the very Anglo-Saxon name of "Walter." At the start of this play, Walter Warner is aloof and condescending. Challenged by Morris, Walter begins to reconsider his ideas about the function of art. Then, the change becomes broader and deeper. Walter becomes a more relaxed, more open, warmer individual.

Is this implausible? I don't think so. First, Morris is a strong persuader. And he doesn't merely argue. Morris will pay for the dog he wants added to the painting. Walter is gradually moved by Morris' strong love for his wife.

Second, we see just a bit of dissatisfaction in Walter that is fertile soil for change. He acknowledges that he has not connected with other people as much as he should have. He is ready to catch up now. Even Walter's appreciation for the beauty of the natural world seems to have dulled. Whereas Morris is enthusiastic about the view from Manawontic Beach, to Walter it's just "OK." The surprise is that Walter's change spurs a change in Morris. He will try to moderate the impulse to argue (which I share) that has too often gotten him into trouble.

Arguing Jews

My father was studying law in night school when the Great Depression hit in 1929. (Back then, you didn't need to attend law school to become an attorney.) The prospects for freshly minted attorneys were suddenly very dim, and so Al became a salesman. Truly, he was cut out for higher-level work than traipsing through Brooklyn and Newark calling on customers to sell furniture.

Al Farkas relished a carefully constructed argument just as he enjoyed a well-told story. He often set up dinner-hour debates with my brother and me (me especially because I was the older son). "Should the Communist Party be outlawed?" "Should the serial rapist Caryl Chessman—who never killed anyone—be sentenced to death?" Mitchell and I got to choose which side to take, but Al expected reasonable knowledge of current events and solidly constructed arguments. When I discovered the debate club in high school, I thought to myself, "I've been doing this all my life."

Later, when Al and I argued about the Vietnam War, it was not for the sport and pleasure of it. There was harsh disagreement. He subscribed staunchly to the "domino theory," which meant fighting the encroachment of Communism anywhere in the world. Furthermore, he did not believe that college kids had the depth of knowledge to challenge the rooms full of Pentagon and State Department foreign affairs professionals who believed that the war was necessary and winnable. But Al had raised an arguer, and a football stadium full of Cold War experts was not going to stop me from opposing the Vietnam War.

Butterflies

A 10-minute play by

David K. Farkas

Setting:

The office of Dr. Alan Aronowitz, a psychiatrist in present-day Boston.

Characters:

Dr. Alan Aronowitz: A psychiatrist with the manner of an East Coast Jew. May be played with any gender presentation. The name "Alanah" might be used

Dr. Robert Epstein: A psychiatrist with the manner of an East Coast Jew.

Mr. Farrell: Dr. Aronowitz's patient.

[Scene 1]

DR. ARONOWITZ is sitting at his desk. There is a second, more comfortable chair for patients, along with a side table. ARONOWITZ wears a sport jacket, and necktie. He stands and walks to the door of his waiting room. He opens the door and motions to someone.

DR. ARONOWITZ: Mr. Farrell. Please come in.

MR. FARRELL enters and looks around. As he does so, he is shooing small moving objects away from his chest and face. ARONOWITZ points to the comfortable chair.

DR. ARONOWITZ: Please take a seat.

FARRELL takes a seat, as does ARONOWITZ. FARRELL does not cease his shooing motions. ARONOWITZ takes up a notebook and pen. He will occasionally take a few notes.

DR. ARONOWITZ: Good to meet you. Tell me, what brings you here today?

MR. FARRELL: I want you to help me get rid of these butterflies. They never leave me alone. No one sees them but me. My wife thinks I'm nuts. At work, I've been put on report. I'm an electrical engineer with Raytheon.

DR. ARONOWITZ: You tell your colleagues about the butterflies?

MR. FARRELL: Of course not. I have my reputation to protect.

DR. ARONOWITZ: Then why are you on report?

MR. FARRELL: My coworkers said the way I act is stressful for them. All my hand motions.

DR. ARONOWITZ: I see.

MR. FARRELL: I knew better than to tell them about my butterflies. Instead I've come to you so you can get rid of them.

DR. ARONOWITZ: I must tell you that I don't see any butterflies. Just your hands moving.

MR. FARRELL: You are the most expensive psychiatrist I could find in Boston. If you can't see the butterflies, where do I go? Should I find someone at Harvard?

DR. ARONOWITZ: Perhaps you shouldn't be looking for a therapist who shares your conviction that you are surrounded by butterflies. Perhaps we should consider the possibility that the butterflies aren't real.

MR. FARRELL: Aren't real? They are right here.

DR. ARONOWITZ: How many do you see?

MR. FARRELL: Right now, six. Sometimes there are as many as nine. Never less than four. Even if I am walking outside or jogging, there are always four or five. They are so annoying. Often they fly right up close to my face. It's a big problem when I'm at the computer. It's even worse when I'm driving.

DR. ARONOWITZ: Do they land on you?

MR. FARRELL: Well, mostly they flutter around me. They like to brush me with their wings. If they land, it's just for a moment. They make it hard for me to sleep. I pull the covers completely over my head. But they always find some little opening. They are really good at this.

DR. ARONOWITZ: I can appreciate your distress, Mr. Farrell . . . Let's assume that there *are* butterflies—real butterflies—surrounding you. Why do you think they've appeared?

MR. FARRELL: How would I know? Isn't that your job? If you can figure out why they are here, you may be able to figure out how to get rid of them.

DR. ARONOWITZ: Actually I don't think that's exactly my job. Looking at the big picture, I think my job is to help you be a happier, more successful person.

MR. FARRELL: I would be a happier person without the butterflies, Dr. Aronowitz. I promise you.

DR. ARONOWITZ: Mr. Farrell, would you work with me and just imagine, just consider the possibility that there are no butterflies.

MR. FARRELL: Why would I do that?

DR. ARONOWITZ: Let's pass on the why. Just try it.

MR. FARRELL continues to shoo away the butterflies.

MR. FARRELL: OK, I'm imagining that these damn butterflies aren't here. Now what?

DR. ARONOWITZ: I'm sorry, that's not exactly what I meant. I know that you see them. I didn't mean that I wanted you to *pretend* that you're not seeing them. Instead, let's assume that they are illusional—not real—and then look for possible reasons. How long have you experienced these butterflies?

MR. FARRELL: They've been with me for about three months. About all a person can possibly stand, wouldn't you agree?

DR. ARONOWITZ: *(Nods in assent.)* . . . What was going on in your life three months ago? Did anything unusual take place?

MR. FARRELL: I don't remember anything special at all.

DR. ARONOWITZ: Hmmm. What events in your past might have caused this? Did you have any significant experiences with butterflies growing up? Were you ever frightened by butterflies?

MR. FARRELL: Who could be frightened by butterflies? I said that they are extremely annoying, not frightening.

DR. ARONOWITZ: Yes, Yes . . . Do you ever dream about butterflies?

MR. FARRELL: No, I try *not* to dream about them. Actually when I finally fall asleep, I have normal dreams—or maybe I don't dream. I really don't know.

> ARONOWITZ exhibits frustration and befuddlement. He has no clue how to proceed.

DR. ARONOWITZ: Hmmm. There are various possibilities to be explored, and that is what we will do. Yes. Yes, indeed.

> ARONOWITZ glances very obviously at his watch. He is "saved by the bell."

DR. ARONOWITZ: Mr. Farrell, I see that our session is about over. I think we're off to a good start.

MR. FARRELL: We are? You have some ideas? Do you have a plan to get rid of my butterflies?

> ARONOWITZ pauses for a long time in his uncertainty. But then an idea crosses his mind. It is so strange, so radical, it startles him.

DR. ARONOWITZ: Actually, I do . . . I would like to invite another psychiatrist to join us at our next meeting—Dr. Robert Epstein. I think he might have some insights that can help us. Dr. Epstein is a psychiatrist, but he is also deeply immersed in Talmudic Studies and the central work of Jewish mysticism, the Kabbalah.

MR. FARRELL: Sounds very impressive. Do I pay extra for this fellow?

DR. ARONOWITZ: Well, yes. You do.

MR. FARRELL: That's OK. If you don't have any answers for me, I want to meet with someone who does.

DR. ARONOWITZ: Then that's how we will proceed. I'll see you this time next week.

MR. FARRELL: OK. I'll be here.

ARONOWITZ stands, followed by FARRELL. ARONOWITZ ushers FARRELL to the door.

DR. ARONOWITZ: Goodbye. Nice meeting you, Mr. Farrell.

ARONOWITZ makes a gesture that combines frustration with hope. He may look skyward.

[Scene 2]

Again we are in DR. ARONOWITZ'S office. EPSTEIN and ARONOWITZ are seated in chairs similar to ARONOWITZ'S in Scene 1. EPSTEIN wears a jacket and tie. ARONOWITZ wears a loosened tie, and his sport jacket is hung on a chair or is otherwise visible.

DR. EPSTEIN: Treat a patient with Jewish mysticism? Where did you get such a crazy idea? I have a standard practice, just like you. My interest in the Talmud and the Kabbalah is personal, not professional.

DR. ARONOWITZ: Yes, I know. But I was stumped by this guy and his weird problem. Then, in a moment, just as the session was ending, I got this wild idea. You're my wild idea. Will you do it?

DR. EPSTEIN: I have strong reservations about this, but as a friend, I'll go along. Do you want me to wear a yarmulke or a tallit?

DR. ARONOWITZ: Maybe just a yarmulke. But not just one of those simple black ones or white ones. Find a more exotic looking yarmulka. And try to sound Jewish.

DR. EPSTEIN: I am Jewish.

DR. ARONOWITZ: Try to sound more Jewish.

DR. EPSTEIN: Alan, I'm not sure we should be doing this. Your plan departs from all accepted psychiatric theories. And it's unethical. We're deceiving a patient, resorting to trickery.

DR. ARONOWITZ: Our motive is good.

DR. EPSTEIN: That's not enough. That doesn't make it ethical.

DR. ARONOWITZ: Well, if it works, we'll have a story no other psychiatrists can tell.

DR. EPSTEIN: I won't tell that story until I'm safely retired.

DR. ARONOWITZ: Maybe we can write this up as a case study. If you're skittish, we can use pseudonyms.

DR. EPSTEIN: For what journal? *The New Age Journal of Off-the-Wall Psychiatric Research?*

[Scene 3]

In ARONOWITZ'S office, ARONOWITZ and EPSTEIN are seated in the office chairs. There is an ornate, be-jeweled box on the table. Both men wear sport jackets and ties. In addition, EPSTEIN wears an exotic yarmulke and exhibits a more Jewish manner than in the previous scene. FARRELL is seated in the patient's chair, nearest to EPSTEIN. He continues to shoo away his butterflies.

DR. ARONOWITZ: Mr. Farrell, this is Dr. Epstein. I have familiarized him with your case.

EPSTEIN gazes at FARRELL'S butterflies. He tracks their movements closely with his eyes.

DR. EPSTEIN: What beautiful butterflies! They must be monarchs?

MR. FARRELL: You can see them! Yes, I think they are monarchs.

DR. EPSTEIN: Monarchs are an endangered species.

MR. FARRELL: I don't care that monarchs are an endangered species. *(Points to the butterflies fluttering around him.)* How do we get rid of them?

DR. EPSTEIN: Get rid of them? They are very beautiful, delicate creatures, totally harmless.

MR. FARRELL: Well, yes. I guess that's true. How come you can see them? No one else ever has.

EPSTEIN stands. He quickly signals the audience that a deception is about to begin. He begins his next speech in an intense and expansive manner but gradually returns to a more normal tone of voice.

DR. EPSTEIN: The Kabbalah contains knowledge very different from the materialistic physics that governs modern thought. The Kabbalah tells us that what we see depends on our spiritual state. And I have just enough of a connection to the transcendental realm to see your butterflies. Actually I can only see them when you and I are together. If you walked out of the room, I wouldn't see them.

EPSTEIN sits.

MR. FARRELL: If I walked out of the room, they would follow me.

DR. EPSTEIN realizes he has said something stupid and is chagrined.

DR. EPSTEIN: Well, yes. Of course . . . Mr. Farrell. Would you allow me to put my Talmudic study to use, right here, right now? The results will be immediate and, I think, surprising.

MR. FARRELL: I guess so. That's why Dr. Aronowitz brought you in.

DR. EPSTEIN now reverentially removes a vintage Jewish prayer book (or approximation thereof) from the box.

MR. FARRELL: That looks very old.

DR. EPSTEIN: Yes, it is.

EPSTEIN stands and, holding the book with its spine on the right, he opens it to a page he has apparently chosen in advance. EPSTEIN looks down intently on a page and reads something silently to himself. Then he sets the book down on the table. Then he turns to face FARRELL. With sweeping gestures, EPSTEIN draws the butterflies to his own lap. He clearly enjoys their presence. FARRELL ceases to shoo away butterflies. He is delighted.

MR. FARRELL: Yes! That's extraordinary.

ARONOWITZ now displays a birdcage from where it has been concealed. He sets it down on the side table that is between him and EPSTEIN.

DR. EPSTEIN: They are lovely creatures, but it is certainly inconvenient to have them at close quarters. *(Points to cage.)* The butterflies will be very comfortable here.

EPSTEIN opens the door of the cage and guides the butterflies through the open door. Finally, he closes the door. Then he glances at ARONOWITZ and chuckles at the private joke that he and ARONOWITZ are about to share.

DR. EPSTEIN: *(More or less privately to ARONOWITZ.)* This is what we Freudians call "transference." *(Now to FARRELL.)* We have given the butterflies a new home. *(Looks again at ARONOWITZ.)* We've transferred them, so it's transference. *(Back to FARRELL.)* Now you can fully enjoy these delightful little creatures, but they won't annoy you. Also you can leave them at home when you go to work.

MR. FARRELL: Wonderful! Wonderful!

DR. ARONOWITZ: You can go back to living a normal life.

EPSTEIN sits.

DR. FARRELL: *(To EPSTEIN.)* I am so pleased. How do I take care of them? How do I feed them?

DR. EPSTEIN: Very simple.

EPSTEIN points inside the cage to a small plate with fruit slices. There is also a small glass dish with water.

DR. EPSTEIN: See what's on that plate? They love fruit. The fruit must be ripe. Also, they enjoy dipping their wings in a shallow dish of clean water.

MR. FARRELL: That's easy. Do I need to clean the cage?

EPSTEIN is caught off guard. Distressed, he looks to ARONOWITZ, but then improvises.

DR. EPSTEIN: No. That's not necessary. Just replace the fruit when it spoils.

MR. FARRELL: Certainly. This is wonderful. I am so impressed, Dr. Epstein. But I have a question for you. Why did the butterflies appear in the first place?

DR. EPSTEIN: This will be a personal rather than a professional answer. The butterflies are perhaps a gift from God. Your reward for being a good person. You just didn't know how to enjoy this gift.

MR. FARRELL: I don't know. I don't think I've been a good person.

DR. ARONOWITZ: Maybe you've been better than you think.

MR. FARRELL: Not likely. I cheated my brother out of his part of our parents' estate. I'm often harsh and unfeeling toward my wife. I've never given a dollar to charity unless I was shamed into it.

DR. EPSTEIN: Hmmm. Well, sometimes God gives us gifts as a kind of down payment, as an advance on future good behavior. You've gotten your reward in advance. Now you can show God you're worthy of it.

MR. FARRELL: If I don't mend my ways, do I lose the butterflies?

DR. ARONOWITZ: Perhaps worse than that. God gave you a gift expecting you to reciprocate. He might not like your refusal to reform. Remember, I'm speaking personally here, not as a psychiatrist.

MR. FARRELL: OK. I will do better. I'm grateful to God, and I want to keep those lovely butterflies. I will work hard to show God that I deserve them.

DR. ARONOWITZ: Well, Mr. Farrell, all this lies completely within your power. As Freud said, "Be the change you want."

EPSTEIN gets the joke—such a statement is not at all Freudian.

MR. FARRELL: Should I tell my wife?

DR. ARONOWITZ: This is a delicate situation. She will see you caring for butterflies that she is unable to see. This may distress her. She may resent the fact that God chose to show his favor to you and not to her.

MR. FARRELL: Yes, I can see that it might.

DR. ARONOWITZ: Perhaps, with your permission, I can explain all this to her in a way that she can understand. Ideally, I would do this before you get home with the cage and the butterflies. May I phone her as soon as you leave my office? I'll explain *everything*.

MR FARRELL: Yes, that would be helpful. Thank you. Dr. Epstein, you are a brilliant man. Dr. Aronowitz, you brought in someone who could do what you couldn't. You deserve credit for that.

>   ARONOWITZ exhibits irritation at this left-handed compliment.
>   EPSTEIN grins privately at ARONOWITZ.

DR. ARONOWITZ: Thank you, Mr. Farrell. One more thing. Dr. Epstein and I will ask you to make a donation to the charity of your choice instead of paying us.

MR. FARRELL: OK. Sure. But why is that?

DR. ARONOWITZ: We would prefer not to have these two meetings take the form of paid clinical practice. I think the meetings have been highly productive, but our methods definitely departed from accepted standards of clinical practice, so we prefer that this be an informal engagement with a patient, perhaps a kind of research.

MR. FARRELL: Sure. Whatever. I will make a generous donation. Maybe to an environmental organization that preserves butterfly habitat.

DR. ARONOWITZ: An excellent idea, Mr. Farrell. I am so pleased our treatment worked so well for you. If you experience any further problems, we can always resume sessions.

>   ARONOWITZ stands and signals that the session is ending. FARRELL
>   stands to leave. EPSTEIN stands and lifts the cage for FARRELL to take.

DR. EPSTEIN: Don't forget your butterflies.

MR. FARRELL: Goodbye, Dr. Epstein, Dr. Aronowitz. Thank you so much!

>   FARRELL exits.

DR. EPSTEIN: How did we do?

DR. ARONOWITZ: I think we did OK. It was crazy, but it all seems to have worked.

DR. EPSTEIN: Permanently?

DR. ARONOWITZ: Who knows? But I'm hopeful. We did put the fear of God into him, so to speak.

> EPSTEIN gestures near his lap and chest as though he's aware of fluttering insects. Then he gestures frantically.

DR. ARONOWITZ: Bob! What's the problem?

DR. EPSTEIN: God is punishing us for our deception—and for using a holy text to do it. Can't you see these hornets?

DR. ARONOWITZ: Don't be ridiculous. There are no hornets! I don't see anything at all. The hornets you see are just a delusion, a guilt response.

DR. EPSTEIN: No! No! They're all around me. They're all around you too.

DR. ARONOWITZ: I have a solution, Bob. Just hold on tight.

> ARONOWITZ opens his desk drawer *[or perhaps a briefcase]* and shoos the imaginary hornets inside. Then he closes the drawer.

DR. ARONOWITZ: There now. Is that better?

DR. EPSTEIN: Yes, yes, it is! I think they're gone.

DR. ARONOWITZ: Well, OK. If God thought to punish us, he didn't work too hard at it. Your hornets are safely in my desk drawer *[briefcase]*, and that's where I'll leave them. Bob, I really appreciate your help with Mr. Farrell.

The End

Postscript to "Butterflies"

Although "Butterflies" is a goofy comedy, it looks closely at Jewish ethical traditions (See the mini-essay in the postscript to "The Expulsion from Eden"). Dr. Aronowitz follows pragmantic, consequentialist ethics. He is comfortable deceiving Mr. Farrell because the end justifies the means. He even frightens Farrell with the prospect of divine punishment if Farrell doesn't improve his behavior.

In contrast, Dr. Epstein takes a strict deontic stance. God does not want us to lie. (The Ninth Commandment—the one about not bearing false witness—is widely interpreted as prohibiting lying.) Epstein does not, as would many Jews, allow himself an exemption because the lie is a "white lie." Finally, from the standpoint of virtue ethics (the third major framework of ethical thought), both men are admirable. Both are honorable individuals whose goal is to help Farrell.

In its last moments, "Butterflies," like many comedies, shifts into implausibility. Now it is Epstein who complains that he is plagued by insects. Furthermore, these are hornets, not harmless butterflies. Because he is deeply rooted in deontic ethics, Epstein is convinced that God is punishing him for deceiving Farrell and doing so by means of a holy text. So, once again, Aronowitz resorts to beneficent trickery, and once again beneficent trickery solves the problem. The play, we see, endorses consequentialist ethics over Epstein's rigidly deontic ethical stance.

Afterword

Putting together this volume has been an intellectual and emotional journey in which I re-thought my relationship to Judaism and my Jewish ancestry. My initial goals were narrow and modest. Noticing that I'd written quite a few Jewish plays, it made sense to collect them into a single volume. I thought little about the commentary I might offer on each of the plays or what kind of introductory material I might write.

I now find myself more deeply Jewish than before. I think much more about the varying conditions of Jewish life throughout the diaspora and, especially, about the immigrant generations in the United States. I have a more sympathetic understanding of seemingly archaic Jewish practices such as maintaining two sets of dishes and utensils (one for meat and one for dairy), as my mother-in-law had done.

I regret the harsh and stupid Hebrew school education that was inflicted on me—two afternoons each week following regular school—in the years preceding my bar mitzvah. I understood my bar mitzvah to be the end of this unpleasantness and, more generally, my ticket *out of* further religious observance. Once again, there are contradictions: My parents cared a great deal about how well I would chant my haftorah and the associated blessings (I had private lessons from the cantor), but they raised no objection to my adolescent assertion that this would be the end of my Judaism.

While putting together this book, I did more Jewish reading, and I returned to some books I'd read long ago. When I read Bernard Malamud in graduate school, I read him as a graduate student, intent on literary analysis. Now I was reading Malamud and other Jewish authors not as someone engaged in literary study or even as a general reader, but as a Jew. I looked for direct connections between these books and who I am.

As part of my Jewish reading, I read Irving Howe's masterful *World of Our Fathers* (1976), a history of the immigration to America (primarily New York City) by millions of Jews from Eastern Europe. This book strengthened my emotional connection to my grandparents and my Eastern European forebears, about whom I know little.

My mother's father was born in a provincial town, but became a clerk in a clothing store in Kiev and then a corporal in the Czar's army, an unusual attainment for a Jew. In New York, he learned to speak fluent English and owned a little candy store which had Gentile as well as Jewish customers. He went to shul regularly and prized his four pretty daughters. I know that later there were a few desperate letters from a relative who, with his family, had stayed behind and who, we presume, died in the Holocaust.

In Hungary, my father's father was a cattle drover, a "cowboy" I tell Jonah and Hazel. In New York, he delivered goods with his own horse and wagon. He apparently liked his schnapps and homemade wine (fermented in big jugs on the fire escape). One of my father's few stories about the man—which he told with comic relish—was that in the evenings, sitting in his living room chair, his father could not distinguish between Al and Harold, the two youngest of his nine children. When they played on the floor, he'd point to one of them and ask Celia, his wife, surely in Yiddish, "Which one is that?"

I never knew my grandparents, except for vague memories of my mother's parents, who died when I was a young boy. Nor did Sally and Al speak much about their parents or what they had heard about life in the Old Country. They had been taught at home to focus on America. Neither learned more than a smattering of Yiddish. But they and my aunts and uncles could have answered many questions. I wished I'd asked them.

I write these paragraphs on the seventh night of Hanukkah (December 4, 2021). Yesterday evening, Jean and I joined my daughter and son-in-law for dinner, a dinner that included their Hanukkah celebration. We lit the Menorah candles, Jean and I sang the blessing, and everyone took an interest in the candles as they burned. Each child received a small gift. My son-in-law, raised Lutheran, asked a few questions about the historical basis of the holiday.

I was more than pleased when Hazel asked me to read her *Hershel and the Hanukkah Goblins* (Kimmel, 1989). We looked together at the illustrations. I feared she would dislike Hershel's very unfamiliar appearance (he is decidedly Eastern European in physiognomy and dress), but she thoroughly enjoyed the book. All during Hanukkah, I attended closely to each indication on the part of Hazel and Jonah that they were definite about their Jewish identity. Even very small things such as their interest in the Jewish origins of the rugelach desert that Jean had brought mattered to me. I hope they decide to learn more as they get older.

Reference List

Aristotle. (1902). *The Poetics*. (S. H. Butcher, Trans.; 3rd edition revised). Macmillan and Co. (Section XIII, pp. 45-47).

Blau, Yitzchak (2000). The implications of a Jewish virtue ethic. *The Torah U-Madda Journal*, Vol. 9, pp. 19-41.

Dorff, Elliot N. & Crane, Jonathan K. (2013). *The Oxford Handbook of Jewish Ethics and Morality.* Oxford University Press.

Frank, Helena (Trans.). (1912). *Yiddish Tales.* The Jewish Publication Society. https://www.gutenberg.org/ebooks/33707. Also available as a free audiobook: https://archive.org/details/yiddish_tales_ap_librivox

Ginzberg, Louis. (2003). *Legends of the Jews.* (Vol 1. 2nd edition) (Henrietta Szold and Paul Radin, Trans.). The Jewish Publication Society.

Howe, Irving. (1976). *World of Our Fathers.* Simon and Schuster.

Huberman, Rabbi Irving. (2018). Why Jews love to argue. Blog post 06/15/2018. https://www.ctionline.org/blogs/rabbi-huberman?post_id=944279.

> A woman who I am currently studying with towards conversion recently posed a question after attending her fiancé's family Seder. "Rabbi – there was so much yelling and interrupting at the table – no one agreed with anyone," she began. "But when the meal came, everything changed. Everyone started laughing and joking with each other. And at the end of the evening – after all the singing – everyone hugged and kissed on the way out the door. "She tilted her head and said, "I don't get it." To which

I replied, "Welcome to Judaism, where arguing is the national pastime." If there is one characteristic which has kept the Jewish people alive for more than three thousand years, it is our love of debate, discussion, and disagreement, and never more evident than at the Seder table. It is in our DNA as much as *Dayenu*. Two Jews, three opinions.

Jewish views on sin. (2021). In Wikipedia. https://en.wikipedia.org/wiki/Jewish_views_on_sin.

> Sins between people are considered much more severe in Judaism than sins between man and God. Yom Kippur, the main day of repentance in Judaism, can atone for sins between man and God, but not for sins between man and his fellow, that is until he has appeased his friend. Eleazar ben Azariah derived [this from the verse]: "From all your sins before God you shall be cleansed" (Book of Leviticus, 16:30) – for sins between man and God Yom Kippur atones, but for sins between man and his fellow Yom Kippur does not atone until he appeases his fellow.

Kimmel, Eric. (1989). *Hershel and the Hanukkah Goblins*. Illustrations by Trina Schart Hyman. Holiday House.

Pinsker, Sanford. (1971). *"The Schlemiel" as Metaphor*. Studies in Yiddish and American Jewish Fiction. Southern Illinois University Press.

Pinsker writes:

According to the Universal Jewish Encyclopedia, a schlemiel "handles a situation in the worst possible manner or is dogged by an ill luck that is more or less due to his own ineptness."

www.ingramcontent.com/pod-product-compliance
Lightning Source LLC
Chambersburg PA
CBHW051139020726
47501CB00005B/1587